CLORIS HUGHES

A NOVEL BY

STEPHEN TANNENBAUM

Red Engine Press
Pittsburgh, Pennsylvania

Library of Congress Control Number: 2019934431

ISBN: 978-1-943267-61-3 Trade paperback
ISBN: 978-1-943267-62-0 Ebook

Printed in the United States.

Red Engine Press
Pittsburgh, PA

THE AUTHOR WISHES TO:

Dedicate this novel to his mentor of many years, now deceased, Monty Culver, Professor Emeritus of English Writing, University of Pittsburgh.

And to his wife, Shirley, who saw the potential for this work even before the author did himself.

And wishes to thank his first readers, Riv Swartz and Diane Rudov, for their tireless efforts on behalf of the work.

CLORIS HUGHES

A NOVEL

CHAPTER 1

Cloris Hughes

The front door buzzer buzzed, but Cloris Hughes's mind was elsewhere.

Oh, yes, she knew her man, knew just where she would find her husband's shirt—his dry-clean-only shirt. The hamper in the laundry room. Thinking that, she finished dressing.

These words of wisdom her mother, Katherine Schermer, had confided to the teenage Cloris, whose father had abandoned them and later had been killed in the War:

"If you want to find evidence of a cheating husband, Cloris, examine his shirt collars."

Cloris understood that her mother was a bitter, spiteful woman who had lost her foothold on the world; a struggling, unhappy wanderer whose world had crumbled beneath her feet. Katherine was in the habit of wandering aimlessly around the room as if she were lost, often lost in an alcoholic fog, an ugly blue vein throbbing, threatening to burst in the middle of her forehead.

This was more of mother's wisdom:

"At some point in an affair the husband—the louse—will calculate in his little pea brain what a divorce is going to cost, and, overwhelmed, he hesitates to act. Frustrated by this, the homewrecker will decide to mark him. Brand him as if he were a steer or a stallion. Why? I'll tell you why, Cloris. To warn you, the unwitting wife, to get out of the way, another woman is taking possession."

According to Katherine, Jack Schermer, Cloris's father, had abandoned them shortly after Cloris was born. But gratefully the son-of-a-bitch had died in the War.

Everything Cloris knew of her father originated with Katherine and according to her, all things hurtful, painful, injurious, even evil, were personified in Jack Schermer. Such bitter stuff had been Cloris's daily diet.

She was determined to prevent divorce from sullying her own marriage; she vowed as much to herself. But she couldn't help categorizing her mother as the typical, forsaken woman. Venomous, vengeful, unreliable. But now she wondered if her mother had been right.

Again, the front door buzzer buzzed.

Cloris dragged herself to the bathroom to wash a

located, as were two others she found last week and the week before, where the collar of a man's shirt would rest against the right side of his neck.

The nasty bitch had branded Cloris's husband with the tip of a finger, moistened with her perfume while at the same time she was placing her lips—*and maybe the tip of her tongue*—to the right side of his treacherous neck. *She is helping herself to my husband and she wants me to know.*

Furious. Another buzzer went off, this time accompanied by vibrations in the right butt pocket of her jeans—her cell phone. Furious. She might have hurled it through the glass slider. Breathed deeply. Held it to her ear.

"It's me, Missus Hughes, Mattie. I rang the bell but no answer. You hear, Missus Hughes? It's me."

Bruno Maestromateo, the gardener. So used to his customers calling him Mattie, he does it himself. A man of average height, wire thin and wire tough, thick black hair under a *Burpee's* ballcap, and a penchant for wearing bib overalls, making him look like a farmer. An Italian farmer, American born, but with a dash of oregano in his speech.

He told Cloris, having received no response to the doorbell, he returned to his truck and was calling her from there.

"I'm here now, Missus Hughes. Out front in a my truck."

What timing. Cloris breathed deeply, trying to calm herself. She told him to come around back, she'd meet him in the garden.

There was an 8 x 12-foot concrete patio behind the house, furnished with an ancient glider and a glass-topped dining table with four wrought iron chairs. Beyond the patio was the garden, neither too big nor too small for an urban garden. An expanse of lawn was terraced with a low wall of red brick.

Enclosing the lawn in a wide arc were lush beds of purples and pinks, yellows and blues; irises, corydalis, lilies, geraniums and petunias. At the edge of the property just beyond the flower beds: on the right a tall viburnum, the leaves of which changed to red with the changing seasons, but were now dark green and its branches bursting with clumps of tiny red berries. At the center edge, an oak-leafed hydrangea that sported pink and blue blossoms the size of snowballs.

However, Mattie the gardener had come today to see the object on the left—a single tree less than eight feet tall, a yew, a supposed evergreen but whose needles looked wearily, sadly brown.

Mattie entered by way of a stone path that led along the north side of the house, at the end of which was an old-fashioned, wire gate that opened to the garden. Cloris came through the game room's glass slider then crossed the patio and the lawn. They arrived simultaneously at the site of the desiccated yew. Words of greeting seemed somehow inappropriate.

Each used a hand to shield his and her eyes from the low morning sun; they appeared to be saluting the sad looking thing. An observer, had there been one, might have expected to hear a bugle call.

Merda!

Mattie considered this to be his failure. He was descended from a long line of distinguished university professors from Salerno, Sicily, hence the Maestro-part of his name, but Mattie was most proud to be a gardener, proud of his ability to make things grow. He claimed not to be superstitious, but at the sight of this dying yew, he was tempted to spit between two fingers.

He eyed Missus Hughes warily and was sorry to see his customer taking it so badly. She looked angry and at the same time he thought she might burst into tears.

Mattie liked Missus Hughes. She treated him fairly and with respect. She was pretty in a quiet, dark way that he found attractive. He thought of her as a little bit of a thing, too short for a tall man like him.

But when she looked up at him, her soft brown eyes seemed to reach out and warm his heart. And he liked that rather than smelling of perfume she always smelled of an expensive soap. Mostly he liked her because she didn't seem to mind getting her hands dirty. But now she looked about to wilt.

"I thought I was being clever," Mattie said, removing his ball cap and scratching behind his right ear. "A yew for Missus Hughes. Huh."

She said, "I wanted it to work. I did what I could, tried so hard."

"I know you did," Mattie said. "Maybe if I tried again? You know, fed it again? Watered it more?" He searched the sky hoping to find dark clouds. "Although we've had lots a rain lately. But maybe…" He shrugged. "Maybe we try to save it?"

"Try to save it? Well… but wouldn't that be whipping a dead horse?" She looked at him for the first time today. "A waste of time?" *Was mother right?*

Mattie felt bad for the poor yew; felt bad for Missus Hughes too. He knew what he would do if the decision were his to make. But condemn the poor thing or attempt to revive it, it was up to Missus Hughes.

For a moment the Earth stood still, then Mrs. Hughes drew a deep cleansing breath and made up her mind.

CHAPTER 2

Accounts Payable

Damn it, I won't give her the satisfaction.

Cloris vowed to not give her vodka besotted hag of a mother the satisfaction of admitting to her that she had been right: right in warning Cloris not to fall in love with a Hughes man (she had done it anyway and married him, and now she had begun to rue the day); Mother had been right as well about checking a suspect husband's shirt collars for traces of 'the other woman' (she had done that, too, and found blots of lipstick and *Love Stain*).

She had once considered her mother's persistent warnings about Hughes men judgmental and prejudicial. They were that still, in Cloris's mind. But as for examining shirt collars for clues, Cloris came up with what she considered a better way, a 20th Century way—in addition to examining his shirt collars, she intended to examine his monthly *Mastercard* statements.

Cloris climbed the stairs and hung a left to the smallest of three bedrooms, a corner room that served them both as an office and doubled as an occasional guest room.

There was a sofa bed whose cushions were upholstered with a beige fabric and wine-colored piping. The windows on each side of the corner that faced the street were draped with fabric that matched the sofa bed. The desk that used to be Reynolds' favorite piece of furniture in his bedroom in Worthington Manor had been transferred here and set in the place of honor near the middle of the room. There was also a waist-high walnut bookcase along one wall, a Turkish rug thrown on the hardwood floor and a metal faux fireplace, chimney-less, in another corner.

Cloris took a seat at the desk and delved into the drawer that had been designated for accounts payable. She found the *Mastercard* statement on top of the pay-by-the-fifteenth pile of bills. The envelope had been slashed open with a sharp letter opener, but the envelope and its contents were otherwise unmolested. No attempt to conceal it. She thought, *The arrogant bastard didn't think he had to.*

There were two pages of entries: retail purchases, a few charitable contributions, restaurant and cocktail lounge charges at places to which Cloris had never been, including a one-night stay at a Ramada Inn. A charge for flowers from *1-800-InterBloom.* Cloris banged her fist on the desktop. *He sent her flowers and used a competitor. The bastard.* She thought the least he could have done was buy them at *Posies*, but then she realized how ridiculous that was. Had she lost her mind? She was afraid she had.

Soon, though, her anger burned out and the stillness of the empty house closed in on her.

Cloris would have strangled Reynolds, if she could have. She wanted to strangle him, if only he were there.

CHAPTER 3

Visiting Mother

In Cloris's opinion, the job of the security guard posted at the entrance to the County Home for Recovery & Rehabilitation ought to be to stop people from going in. Instead some greedy s.o.b. had positioned an ATM cash machine at the entrance, again in Cloris's opinion, as a subtle hint to visitors that attendants inside the building were deserving of tips. Cloris was never in a charitable mood when about to visit her alcoholic curmudgeon of a mother; and she didn't believe in tipping.

Just beyond the ATM machine, a sliding glass door was supposed to automatically open to let people in, but often was stuck closed. Since Cloris wished she didn't have to go in anyway, that didn't bother her. It did bother her when once in a while the door refused to let her out. This morning, it opened to admit her.

She crossed the reception area on her way to the sign-in desk. Despite the use of acoustical tiles on the ceiling and worn throw rugs on the concrete floor, her footsteps echoed.

There was a glass gazebo in the center of the room that housed exotically colored birds, and there was a large bubbling tank for seawater tropical fish. The gazebo hadn't seen a squeegee in a long while, and two of the fish were floating on the surface of the water. There was no one to enjoy them anyway. In Cloris's experience the residents had few visitors. They had so far survived their addictions, but perhaps their friends had not. *So far Mother has survived. My luck.*

She assumed that an incontinent inmate had had an accident in the reception area recently, for the smell of commercial-strength disinfectant was strong. She took the elevator to the fourth floor.

The architect who designed the County Rehab facility had wasted no imagination on it; it was a simple red brick rectangle. On the fourth floor—though Cloris had never visited the other floors, she expected they were identical—each patient's little private space was situated along the outer perimeter of the corridors, affording each a rain-dappled, soot-streaked window to the outside. The common areas, such as the TV room, dining room and the nursing station, were centrally located.

Cloris stepped out of the elevator to be confronted by the supervisor of the fourth floor, Debra LePage.

Debra had acquired the nickname DoubleWide Debbie, and they called her that behind her back.

She wasn't all that wide, Cloris had seen wider women. But those women were fat, whereas DoubleWide Debbie, with muscular shoulders and biceps like a linebacker and legs like the ones on the grand piano in Cloris's living room, DoubleWide Debbie was fiercely imposing. She had hair that remained stubbornly coal-black despite her middle age.

Rumor had it that DoubleWide's hair was afraid to turn gray; afraid of what she would devise to punish the hair if it dared turn gray. With all that came a fearful disposition, she was an even thornier woman than Cloris's mother. DoubleWide was a permanent fixture of the Rehab facility, actually the most tenured employee in the building. Not because of skill and efficiency, but because of her size and disposition no one had the courage to fire her. She was truly a frightening sight lumbering toward Cloris, extra, extra-large, blue surgical scrubs and all; it was all Cloris could do just to stand her ground.

Near the end of a nose that looked as if it had been mashed in a fist fight, DoubleWide balanced a pair of wire-rimmed glasses with tiny round lenses. They made her face look disproportionately wide, but they did nothing for her vision. She didn't recognize Cloris even when she came close to trampling on her.

"Well now," she said. "Ain't you a welcome sight on a dreary day."

"It's not dreary, Miss LePage," Cloris said. "It's a gorgeous day."

"That's out there, we're in here."

Up close to her—it was the first time Cloris had been this close—DoubleWide's face was baby-bottom smooth, with deep folds at the corners of her mouth. She was either grinning at Cloris or suffering the pain of gastric distress. Either way, the effect was chilling.

Cloris said, "It's Cloris Hughes, Miss LePage. Katherine Schermer's daughter."

"I knew that. I'd recognize you anywhere. Who else dresses as nice as you? Just look at you. Ain't you a sight."

Being in the mood for a little shopping and hoping to coerce her husband into taking her to lunch, Cloris had taken extra care dressing that morning. She put on the pale gray skirt she bought at *Neiman Marcus*, coordinated it perfectly with a mauve tunic with mid-sleeves and belted waist. She wore her best pearls, designer heels and matching bag. She looked splendid, but she doubted Double Wide meant a compliment.

"How's my mother doing today?" Cloris asked, thinking, *She has no idea.*

After a few moments' delay DoubleWide said that Cloris's mother was fine, sweet, and sober as ever. That settled it for Cloris. She backed away from DoubleWide and started up the corridor toward her mother's room.

DoubleWide called after her, "She's not in her room, she's watching TV."

The only thing Katherine Schermer ever watched was the soap, *General Hospital.* Cloris knew it was nowhere near time for that, but the TV room was on the way, so she turned in there.

A large flat-screen TV was mounted on the wall opposite the door, guarded on both sides by floor-to-ceiling windows with venetian blinds drawn against the sun's glare and black iron bars. There were rows of upholstered chairs in front of the TV, but most of the floor space served as a parking lot for walkers and wheelchairs.

Slouched in the wheelchairs were a dozen ladies and men of a wide range of ages, some gray-haired and balding, others young but apparently no more alert. A few of them were schmoozing, most of them were snoozing with the TV droning in the background, mostly ignored. Behind the only table in the room, an attendant was dressed in green scrubs. She slouched over the table, using her arms as a pillow, and snoring.

"Is my mother here? Is Katherine Schermer here?"

Cloris's loud call roused the attendant. She gaped at Cloris; recognized her.

"It ain't one o'clock yet, is it, Ms Hughes? No, it ain't. So, no, Miz Katherine ain't here. This here's *Fox News.*"

Cloris said, "Mother doesn't like *Fox News.*"

"Your mother don't like no news, period."

Cloris agreed, thanked the attendant and moved on.

As she passed the dining room, Cloris saw the rubble of breakfast dishes and soiled paper trash being removed from 4-seater and 8-seater round tables, and the same tables being re-set for lunch by a group of women volunteers. They chatted, laughed as they worked. Cloris continued on.

She stood in the open doorway of her mother's so-called suite. It was one single room, longer than wide, arranged as a bedroom with tiny bath on one side, sitting room on the other. The same architect who had wasted no imagination on the building's design had envisioned an accordion-style divider separating the two areas, but the divider had never been installed.

The furniture, all of it—bed, end tables, sofa, coffee table, lamps—each piece crammed into the tiny space was an émigré from mother's house. The house on Harrison Avenue in which Cloris had spent her early years. Neither she nor her mother had ever been happy in that house. Merely standing at the threshold of the little space made Cloris catch her breath against a pain in her chest like indigestion.

Katherine Schermer had wheeled herself over to the window and was staring at the distant view, her back to the door. Cloris was familiar enough with that view, having stood at that window on more than one occasion: she remembered a deep ravine; and within the ravine, two stretches of deciduous trees heavily in leaf separated by a two-lane asphalt road and a railroad right-of-way with one lonely track; mostly what she remembered was a small foundry abandoned to rust. A pathetic sight.

Katherine's haggard face was reflected in the window pane; Cloris noticed that her mother was not staring down into the ravine, but up at the sky.

Without turning away from the window, Katherine said to Cloris's reflection in the window glass, "My, don't you look nice, all dressed up." She released the brakes of her wheelchair and turned to her daughter. There was a tube feeding oxygen into her nose; her breathing seemed labored. Her skin had a yellowish cast. She said, "Wearing your best pearls, I see. Is it an occasion? Not this visit, I'm sure."

"Hello, mother. You're looking...well." *Awful.* "I'm curious. What's so fascinating outside your window?"

For the longest time Katherine had been staring at the clouds, watching their slow, steady drift, and wondering where they were headed.

"You know," she said, "if you stare at the clouds long enough, huh, you start to feel as if they're carrying you along with them, wherever they are going, you are going. Then you gain vision and you can see, huh, far off, even into the future. As if you were gazing into a crystal ball."

Cloris asked, "And what do you see in that crystal ball?"

"My death." Katherine read the effect that had on

her daughter's face, and she cackled. "You don't like talking, huh, about my death, Cloris?"

"I don't and I won't. If you persist, I'm out of here."

"I'd rather talk about my death, huh, than what you want to talk about. For the umpteenth time, huh, I won't leave this place. My friends are here. I like it here."

"You don't have any friends and you know it. There are so many nicer places, cleaner places with better food, better staffing..."

"A better class of people," Katherine said, flapping her wrist in a hoity-toidy way. "And more expensive."

"But, mother," Cloris pleaded, "we have money, lots of money, why shouldn't you..."

"That's Hughes money." Katherine pounded her fists against the wheelchair armrests. "I'll die before I take, huh, one red cent of Hughes money."

In the dim past before anyone living could remember, the Hughes family –by hook or by crook—had acquired the mineral rights to the entire County: the huge amounts of coal and natural gas; the gold and silver, too, had anyone ever discovered any.

"Do you realize," Katherine said, "if you have a hole in your, huh, pocket and a penny were to fall out, the moment, the very moment that penny hits the ground, huh, it belongs to Malvina Hughes. And her son. Your husband. I hate that, Cloris, I really hate it."

Cloris's fists were clenched at her sides. She wanted to charge at her mother and at the same time wanted to run from her.

She said, "We're back to that again? My having the audacity to marry a Hughes? Now for sure I'm out of here."

She turned and hurried away, with her mother's words echoing after her along the corridor, "Don't say I didn't warn you, Cloris. Don't say, huh, I didn't..."

CHAPTER 4

A Hint of Ash

As if Cloris Hughes' mother, Katherine Schermer, had purposely planned to upstage her daughter, she succumbed to cirrhosis of the liver just days before Cloris's divorce decree was finalized.

Cloris's marriage to Reynolds Hughes took place over her mother's objections. Abandoned by her husband when Cloris was an infant, Katherine was embittered toward the institution of marriage in general, but she was particularly opposed to her daughter's marriage to a Hughes, any Hughes.

Consequently, from the time of the wedding—which Katherine refused to attend—to the time of her sudden catastrophic death, few words passed between mother and daughter; and those few words were, "Cloris, I told you so."

Had Cloris loved her mother? Would she miss her, now that she was gone? Or was she glad to be rid of her? No one present at *Fletcher's Chapel of Rest &*

Crematory could tell, not by looking at her. Cloris showed no emotion that anyone could see. And they were looking.

A handful of sickly-looking women, elderly men wearing ancient, ill-fitting suits and one young man with a very vague look in his eyes, wearing a long-sleeved sweatshirt and a stained tie were conveyed by van from the County Rehab Facility to pay their respects to Katherine Schermer, their fellow resident.

The young man was near to tears as he complained that Katherine was like a mother to him. The others whispered among themselves: Though barely five feet in height Katherine's daughter, Cloris, was a head turner in that snappy little black number she was wearing. But she was showing too much leg. She was too carefully made up, all that mascara for a funeral? Heavens! And that stylish haircut? They thought she had just come from a downtown salon. And not so much as a single tear? Was she chiseled from stone?

What she actually was, she was mortified by the place her mother had chosen for her own funeral. Before its present incarnation as a failing crematory, Fletcher's was a failed *OK Market*, and before that a failed *Felix's Fish & Chips*.

The chapel walls still reeked of dead fish and rotting vegetables. Its windows hadn't seen a squeegee in a decade; they were rain streaked and muddy. All surfaces in the chapel except for the pews—the

mourners' clothing inadvertently dusted the pews—
were covered with a fine beige patina. Who knew,
was it dust or ash from the crematory?

On the wall above the catafalque on which her
mother's casket rested was what Cloris supposed was
the motto of Fletcher's in large gold italic script:

What They Did Is Part of What We Have Become.

Too true.

Cloris imagining her mother, wheelchair bound,
oxygen reliant, and thus forced to hunt for a funeral
home in an out-of-date phone book, imagined her
having a witchingly good cackle when she chose
Fletcher's, knowing her daughter would be mortified
by the place and knowing she would be sticking her
daughter with the bill for the proceedings.

The Rehab inmates told Cloris they were sorry to
see her mother go, yes indeed they would miss her,
they all said, but it was hard for Cloris to tell if they
meant it, said as listlessly as it had been. Prayers
were said listlessly too, as if no one was convinced
any god was listening.

Then a whirring sound, a metallic clang of engag-
ing gears. Cloris watched as the casket that contained
her mother was conveyed slowly, slowly through an
opening in the wall until it was out of sight into the
adjacent room. *Into the incinerator.*

Of course, Cloris assumed she would outlive her
mother; it was the natural order of things. That knowl-

edge should have been a comfort to her, a source of strength in the face of her mother's constant badgering and drunken ridicule.

It should have been a comfort, and it was. But still, once the casket had passed from sight into the crematory, she felt such unexpected relief, such release, as if she had just stepped into a refreshing shower.

Cloris thought she might sneeze. Along with the ghastly odors that exuded from the chapel walls, she felt a hint of ash hanging dryly in the air, tickling her nose.

The residents of the Rehab Facility were herded back to the van by a young woman with a pageboy haircut and dressed modestly in a skirt and loose-fitting jacket of blue serge. Obviously, a nun in the County employ. She checked names on a clipboard as each of her charges struggled up into the van.

Satisfied that all were safely on board, the young woman re-entered the chapel, still carrying her clipboard, and approached Cloris. A large wooden crucifix hung well down on her chest by a silver chain.

Cloris thanked her for coming.

Her name was Sister Esme, she said, and no thanks were necessary, she wouldn't have missed it, she had witnessed many burials, of course, but never a cremation.

"There wasn't much to witness," Cloris replied.

"I can't say I'm sorry about that," Sister Esme said.

"No. Nevertheless, I'm grateful you brought mother's friends."

"Uh, friends…well, yes, I suppose you could call them that."

Cloris nodded and said, "Mother had a sharp tongue."

"Katherine Schermer had a blasphemous tongue, God forgive her. When I questioned your mother's choice of cremation… I knew she wasn't Catholic, but still… She said to me, and I don't know if she really meant it or if she meant to shock me. She said, 'Since me and my liver are bound to burn in hell, I might as well get some practice in.'"

"She would say something like that."

Sister Esme wished the grace of God on Cloris, then returned to her charges. The van immediately departed.

A pair of Schermer cousins and their spouses offered their final condolences and, yes, they said they had remembered to sign the guest book. Cloris had heard tell of them from her mother, but knew not a one of them, had no idea how they had learned of her mother's death, and wasn't curious enough to ask. She was happy to see their backs as they headed for their cars.

The clergyman provided by *Fletcher's*, a man of one denomination or another of Protestantism—mother hadn't cared or specified; nor did Cloris care—any-

sleepless night from her exhausted eyes. She looked in the mirror and saw her mother's face. The haggard image posed a question: *Is this the start of something, or is it the end?*

Downstairs to the laundry room, Cloris lifted the lid of the clothes hamper. There, as expected, was the shirt her husband had worn yesterday to his dental office, then to dinner with colleagues, and after that—so he said—with those same colleagues who dragged him to—of all things—a basketball game at Our Lady of Mercy College. *Yes, sure.*

He owned a half dozen shirts like this one, all of them pale blue, silk shirts—made in China, Cloris read from the label—he preferred their weightless freedom in summer. He wore them accented with a plain, navy-blue tie, with navy trousers and a white, poplin, doctor's coat. *Very neat, very professional, very attractive. Swell.* How many times had she pleaded with him not to toss the shirts in the hamper? That they needed to be drycleaned? *How many times?*

Cloris plucked the shirt from the top of the smelly heap; she hugged it to her breast, buried her face in it.

There was a trace of lipstick on one point of the collar and a spot—still damp—the size of a fingertip near the other point, easily missed except for the fact that the fingertip had been dipped in perfume.

Not a popular scent that Cloris was familiar with, but a musky, darkly sinister and persistent scent she had labeled, HOMEWRECKER. The lipstick trace was

way, the clergyman was lingering around the chapel looking busy, doing nothing. Managing only to soil his black pinstripe suit with beige powder. Or was it ash. Cloris wondered if etiquette demanded that she tip the man. She hoped not, since she had no intention of doing so. She glared at him and he scurried away.

That left Cloris with the only other person remaining in the chapel, a woman whose arrival at the funeral Cloris hadn't noticed and hadn't expected—her almost ex mother-in-law, Malvina Hughes. Almost ex because the divorce had yet to be finalized. It was apparent that Malvina had lingered to have words with her daughter-in-law. Cloris's heart sank.

What in heaven's name would Malvina Hughes be doing here? Cloris doubted Malvina had ever met her mother. Who could have convinced her to present herself in as disreputable a place as *Fletcher's Chapel of Rest & Crematory*? A moment's thought and Cloris knew the answer.

Malvina was coming toward Cloris with the usual determined set to her face, but her steps were cautious, on her toes as if she were negotiating a minefield. Hardly the stride of a powerbroker, who usually acted as if she owned not just the County but the entire planet,

"Mother Hughes."

"Don't look so surprised, Cloris, I'm not here for her," Malvina said, nodding toward the wall behind which the casket had disappeared. "She can burn in hell for all I care. I'm here on a mission." Frown lines from the corners of Malvina's mouth made her appear more pugnacious than ever.

A mean mouth, Cloris thought, *mean as rosebushes*.

Cloris harbored similar feelings toward her husband's mother that she did toward her own. She would gladly see Malvina Hughes trundled toward an incinerator. But she forced a smile and complimented Malvina on her choice of clothing for the occasion, a pencil skirt and matching fitted jacket in a black wool-blend fabric. Expensive. She was tall and nicely built for her age—Cloris guessed Malvina was pushing seventy. She usually wore pastel-colored pantsuits, but Cloris thought she looked good in black. Of course, she'd look without the constant anger.

Cloris said, "A mission. Well, I certainly didn't expect you. You didn't even know my mother, you never met her, did you?"

"I had expected to, at your wedding…"

My wedding? You mean ours, Reynolds' and mine.

"…If only Katherine had bothered to come." Malvina loved saying that, it showed as a gleam in her otherwise impenetrable eyes. "Which she didn't."

From the moment Katherine Schermer's marriage failed, she turned against the institution of marriage. That was why she boycotted the wedding. Cloris saw no good coming from saying that to Malvina. Furthermore, she no longer felt obligated to justify her mother's actions.

Cloris said, "She had her reasons, I'm sure, though I never knew what they were." *Not that you wanted to be there, either.*

Malvina said, "They went into the fire with her."

What a pleasant thought. Thanks, Malvina.

Malvina said, "Reynolds wanted to pay his respects, but he thought his presence might provoke a scene. So, he asked me to attend. In his stead."

In his stead. Lah di dah.

Malvina took a quick step closer to her daughter-in-law, Cloris lurched back in retreat. Malvina had just wanted to not be overheard, though except for the two of them, the chapel was empty.

She said, "Reynolds is willing to come back to you. He still…loves you." She found that incredibly difficult to say. She had always had a better class of woman in mind for her son, but she gritted her teeth and delivered the rest of her message: "With any indication that you're willing to reconcile, he'll come back. He didn't intend divorce, he assured me of that."

She raised a finger dramatically and announced: "There has never been a divorce in the Hughes family. Reynolds would like to try being a faithful husband. He was only doing what he'd seen his father do."

To Cloris, her mother-in-law was making no sense. *Doing what he'd seen his father do? What was that about?* She wished Malvina would leave. Cloris was tired and she had the usual chronic ache in the nape of her neck from having to look up at people. She certainly didn't wish to say anything to provoke further discussion, so she said nothing. That seemed to provoke Malvina even more.

She had turned and had started to leave, but she changed her mind and confronted Cloris again.

"My husband made me miserable our entire married life," she shouted in Cloris's face. "I don't see why it should be any different for you." She turned her back and stomped out of the chapel.

Cloris followed her as far as the chapel door, looked out through the mud streaked glass at the parking lot. The County van was long gone. The Hughes family chauffeur was assisting Malvina into the Hughes family limousine.

CHAPTER 5

A Gentleman's Agreement

*H*ughes men have always had good posture.

Malvina thought this as she poked and prodded her nineteen-year-old son, rearranging the drape of his sweater, tightening the knot of his tie, sweeping a cowlick of hair off his forehead. She wanted him to look just right, he had an appointment to speak with his father. Or might it be more accurate to say, he had an appointment to be spoken to by his father.

It was imprecise to think that Reynolds was afraid of his father, there was too much... stuff in Reynolds for that. But the young man always had been wary of his father.

Broughton R. Hughes II had never been comfortable with children, with his own son in particular. He had no instinct for how to talk to him or how to act with him. Reynolds couldn't remember having ever exchanged an intimacy of any kind with his father. Instead, like gentlemen of acquaintance, they had shaken hands and exchanged formal good wishes; or he had responded with apologies to his father's frowns. An awkward, strained relationship. As if the father had never had a childhood of his own from which to take example. And considering the relationship between Broughton and *his* authoritarian father, perhaps he hadn't.

"There," Malvina said, finally satisfied with his appearance. She patted him, placed a kiss on his forehead. "Now you look every inch a son to be proud of. Off you go to the library, now. Your father is waiting."

"I can't think of a thing I've done to anger P'pah," Reynolds said, hoping that saying it would make it so.

"I'm sure you haven't, dear," Malvina replied. "Your father got a phone call earlier from Edinston Parker…"

"*Dean* Edinston Parker?" Reynolds asked.

"The very same. He and your father were Princeton classmates, you know. Good friends and fraternity brothers, as well. Kappa…something or other."

"Kappa Lambda Mu, M'mah."

"Yes, Kappa Lambda Mu. We've been to a few reunions, though not lately, thank the good Lord." The memory of a herd of old goats acting like kids made Malvina shudder. When she re-focused on her son, he looked worried.

"I think I may have…"

"Stop right there, young man. Whatever you've

done is for your father to hear, not me. I'm not your confessor. To the library with you. Your father awaits."

The library was identical in size and shape to Malvina's sitting room, except it was on the opposite side of the house with no exit to the outdoors. Three of the library's four walls were lined floor to ceiling with custom designed and skillfully carpentered shelves, with railings that curved around the corners to allow one to glide on a single ladder around all three walls in search of that one special book, no matter how high it was perched.

In a child's mind, of course, the ladder allowed a young lad with a proper shove to glide all around the periphery of the library. When father was elsewhere occupied, for it was a verboten act. Having been caught in that act had led to sharp words and a sharp swat on the butt from his P'pah, the only spanking Reynolds recalled ever having received. But ever after that, approaching the library caused shivers of trepidation.

Reynolds always thought the library suited his father's taste—it was so sparsely furnished. Except for the book shelves, the design of which was his grandfather's, not his father's, and the books themselves—such beautifully bound tomes, but also his grandfather's, not his father's. Reynolds doubted his father had read very many of them. There was simply a large teak desk, behind which his father could be found most of the day; the desk looked as if it had once been kicked around badly, but had been rehabilitated. A TV monitor mounted on the wall projected a nonstop stock market feed. A nondescript, vaguely Asian area rug looked as if it was disappointed that its only mission was to cover the bare floor.

In one corner of the room stood an apothecary's cabinet with a hundred tiny drawers that had once held pills and other medicaments, but now accommodated Broughton's stamp collection, the stamps of each country cosseted neatly in its own little drawer. Yes, Broughton was an avid philatelist, having started as a teenager to emulate his hero of the time, Franklin Delano Roosevelt. Eventually, by the age of 30 when the Hughes family business and fortune came under his control, Broughton rejected his hero and the Democratic Party.

There were also two upholstered high-back chairs arranged across from the desk, but the father did not invite the son to take a seat. Nor did he even look up at the young man.

There was a time when Broughton and Reynolds looked more like brothers than father and son. Beside the classic Hughes military posture, they shared the same six-foot height, the same thick brown hair—although the young man wore his over the shirt collar, a length his father could never countenance. They both had straight, aggressive noses and the predatory eyes of eagles, though blue in color and a bit too close together. When a Hughes was looking at you, you felt him looking through you.

There was a time when all that was true, but Reynolds saw now that time had been playing rough with his father. The old man's hair had thinned and grayed, the starch had washed out of his posture, leaving a hunch to his shoulders, and his eyes—in the rare moment when Reynolds could see his eyes, for it seemed Broughton intentionally avoided direct eye contact with his son—they had dulled.

"You asked to see me, P'pah?"

Broughton didn't say that he had, but he must have, for he cleared his throat, looked up finally and said, "Hmm," and nodded.

He told Reynolds that Dean of Men Parker...

His old pal Edinston.

...had called to congratulate him on the academic success of his son's first year. 4.0 in each subject the first semester, and with only a few weeks remaining to complete the second, the same results were expected.

"Congratulations are in order, my, um, boy."

Broughton followed this effusive approbation with what Reynolds decided was a smile, because the corners of his father's mouth moved.

They moved upward, definitely upward.

"Outstanding Scholar, Dean's Especial List. But here, Reynolds, here is what I fail to understand: I cannot reconcile the academic excellence with the other news I received from Edinston, that the Kappa Lambda Mu brothers blackballed you. You're a legacy, for Godsakes, a legacy of two generations. They can't do that, they haven't the right. Well, when I get through reading the Riot Act to those nincompoops in Evanston…"

Reynolds shifted his weight from foot to foot. He said, "Evanston?"

"Illinois, Reynolds, Evanston Illinois, Kappa Lam's national headquarters on the University of Illinois campus. I'll teach those…" This was the first and only head of steam Reynolds had ever seen mounted by his father on his behalf. "Those… I'll teach those fools to blackball a Hughes." The tirade ended with a wheeze.

"But, P'pah, they didn't."

Broughton's left eyebrow twitched.

"They didn't blackball me, sir, I quit…sort of.

"You'll have to excuse me, Reynolds, my hearing…I thought I heard you say, you quit? Sort of?"

He did hear Reynolds say that, and he had. Quit. Sort of. Well, he didn't really quit. He merely refused their offer that he pledge KLM, the fraternity of Hughes men for a century. Reynolds explained to his father that the KLM brothers were not to his taste. Having said that, Reynolds realized he had painted himself into a tight corner, because to say that KLM brothers were not to his taste was to imply that Hughes men—his father and grandfather—were not to his taste either. And as ambivalent as Reynolds was on the subjects of his father and grandfather, this was not the time or place to discuss it.

But the fact remained that the Kappa Lambda Mu brothers were not to Reynolds' taste. By that he didn't mean to imply that they were stupid, only that they were narrow minded. And by that he meant that their compasses were set to an intolerably narrow path.

"I hadn't a thing in common with the Kappa Lams, P'pah. Not that they were ignorant or abusive, perish the thought. They were simply single minded to a fault. Their futures were well in hand, planned to the nth detail: first, of course, completing their studies at Princeton with the highest possible GPA; with that in hand and their families' connections, admittance to Wharton or Darden or Kellogg for that all-important MBA was assured. Then on to Wall Street for a career as hedge fund managers or corporate CFOs. With perhaps an interlude of government service, State Department possibly.

"One's obligatory service to one's Country," Reynolds said, pretending to insert a monocle in his right eye.

Seeing his father was not amused, he went on, "I have nothing against economics and finance, P'pah, but not as a career, not for me. Surely, you've seen I have no interest in it. Not as a career. I want to do something with my hands, P'pah. I want to make something or build something. The Kappa Lams could hardly contain their merriment when I said that. The only things they intend to build are their stock portfolios."

Now Broughton looked even more sadly weighed down than when Reynolds first entered the library. Perhaps the burden of fatherhood had exhausted him beyond his capacity, or perhaps this conversation reminded him of another one he had had long ago with *his* father, and perhaps that conversation was replaying now, almost word for word.

He said, "The Hughes name has been connected with Kappa Lambda Mu for two generations. Is that of no importance to you, Reynolds?"

"The question, P'pah, it seems to me, is, Can I be a Hughes and still be my own man?"

Broughton paused, sighed, decided to let that pass without a reply, as if he should have expected it, or as if he had heard it somewhere before.

He retrieved a magnifying glass and tweezers from a desk drawer and returned his attention to the rare stamp he had been studying. Dismissing his son with a flutter of his fingers.

CHAPTER 6

Cloris Takes a Tour

The latest issue of *Reader's Digest* had been delivered with the morning's mail, and Malvina Hughes thought she might read a few pages of that before retiring for the night. Too drowsy to concentrate on anything heavier. She felt a chill in the October air, so the thought of a warm bed was a pleasant one. She remembered on nights like this her mother—God rest her—would ask their upstairs man, Alcott was his name if she remembered correctly, asked him to set a fire in Malvina's bedroom. Another pleasant memory.

But there were no longer upstairs men, and bedroom fireplaces were no longer of blue-veined marble and they no longer burned real logs. The thought of a gas fireplace tended to rob the image of its romance. Why, Malvina wondered, were there not real fireplaces and why did they not burn real logs?

Why, for that matter, were there no longer upstairs men? Wealth no longer brought the kind of privilege

Stephen Tannenbaum

it did when she was a little girl. *A confusing age, this. Ah, well.*

She rose and was about to climb the stairs to her bedroom when she heard the unmistakable sound of automobile tires crunching their way up the gravel drive toward the house. She thought it was too late for visitors and too early for Reynolds to be returning home from his date. Hearing his key in the front door, Malvina went to meet him in the entrance hall at the foot of the grand staircase.

Reynolds, a junior at Princeton, was home for mid-winter term break. Since the threat of rain and along with it the accompanying threat of October dampness had passed, he had flung his double-breasted London Fog™ raincoat over his right shoulder. He was dressed in a dark brown Harris Tweed coat over a plum-checked shirt, contrasting trousers and sweater vest.

He said, "Oh good, M'mah, you've not gone up yet."

"As you can see. Is anything amiss?"

"No, no. I promised my date a tour of the house. She's a local, so she's seen the outside of the house from the road and she's admired it often. I promised her a tour. If you don't mind, M'mah."

Malvina *did* mind. Not so much that the time was inconvenient, although it *was* inconvenient. Not that she minded being put upon, but she minded that Reynolds knew that she minded and asked her anyway. But what troubled her most was that Reynolds wanted to use the house to impress some common nobody of a girl. Still, she didn't like to disappoint him.

"So," she said, "Where is this local of yours? You didn't leave her stranded in the car? Really, Reynolds, your manners… You mustn't treat a lady, even a common…"

"Now, M'mah, I couldn't very well bring her in without asking, now could I?"

"Oh, very well, bring in the …"

"You won't be short with her?"

"Me, short? The idea, the very idea."

Worthington Manor—the Hughes mansion had been dubbed that by Reynolds' great grandmother—was perched on a sometimes-sunny knoll in the heart of a four-acre lot, fenced, gated and landscaped, off the main road out of the town that was the judicial seat of the County. It was the epitome of the Hughes family pride.

With a glut of sandstone and heavy timbers readily at hand, the architect had indulged his passion for the English Tudor style. Thus, was the family of B. Reynolds Hughes Sr. possessed of a large, beautiful, drafty, 19th century house as uncomfortable to live in as a medieval castle.

B. Reynolds Hughes II, Malvina's now-deceased husband and Reynolds' father, had it completely re-wired, re-plumbed, re-windowed, re-floored, re-insulated, re-everything-ed. So as Cloris Schermer was escorted into Worthington Manor, the Hughes mansion had long ago settled into its beauty and was a pleasure to live in as well, with its Tudor grandeur and its 20th century comfort.

Reynolds helped Cloris past the heavy oak-and-iron door and escorted her into the entrance hall. He expected to find his mother waiting there to inspect the girl, but Malvina was nowhere in sight. Meanwhile Cloris stood at the foot of the grand marble staircase, letting her eyes climb it slowly step by step. Her jaw dropped; all she could say was, "Oh."

Reynolds misunderstood. Turning to the right, and opening what looked like the door to a closet or powder room, he said, "There's an elevator if you don't feel up to the climb."

Elevator? Cloris stared into the space behind the door Reynolds had opened. A cage elevator, sure enough. She gaped at it. Next, she bent her head back to gape at the dizzyingly high vaulted ceiling: ornately etched metal panels and darkly stained arched beams, with a gold-linked chain hanging from one of the beams, and on the end of the gold chain hung a huge crystal chandelier. She gaped at it all and said, "Oh."

Reynolds offered a ride to the upstairs floor in the elevator, but Cloris preferred the stairs. She told Reynolds that she wanted to take the stairs, but really what she wanted to do was to *ascend* them. She thought it would feel as if she were a princess in a fairy tale dressed in a flowing gown ascending a staircase to the stars. Reality came like a slap in the face. Having reached the top and looking back the way she had come, Cloris realized that this wasn't a fairy tale. Had she really ascended? Or had she climbed too high and reached a place where she didn't belong?

In its present configuration, there were four suites on the second floor, each with a bed chamber, luxurious bath, sitting room and large walk-in closet. The master suite was Malvina's alone now that her husband was gone. The second was and always had been Reynolds', now occupied only when Princeton was in recess. And there were two identical guest suites.

"Where does this go?" Cloris asked on discovering yet another staircase, this a narrow one.

"To the Wilps', to the servants' quarters, of course," Reynolds said.

Cloris said, "Oh, but of course."

Across the hall from this stairway was an alcove that was furnished with a dark leather wingchair and an antique table with a white Princess phone.

Reynolds said, "This used to be the upstairs man's station. M'mah found another use for it. What is an upstairs man? Oh, well, back in the day, in my grandfather's day, when there were guests in the house, the upstairs man—sometimes the chauffeur, sometimes another male employee—would be posted here throughout the night. He would act as valet for the male guests, and night watchman, fireplace attendant, that sort of thing. A thing of the past."

Next on Reynolds' agenda was to show off his own private digs, but Cloris declined a tour of the bedroom suites, saying simply that she preferred not to, but feeling that her presence in any of the bedrooms would be an uncomfortable intrusion. Reynolds shrugged; they returned to the ground floor.

By the time they were once again in the entrance hallway, Reynolds had figured out where his mother had gone. He sighed at the inevitability of it. He said, "You'll want to see the sitting room." He led her there.

Sure enough, the sitting room had been arranged like a stage set: The drapes of heavy brocade had been pulled back to expose the French doors, with glass panels that reflected flickering light from the stone fireplace. The gas jets were set to simulate a full, roaring blaze. Malvina was standing imperiously before the fire, Reynolds thought, *playing Queen Victoria.*

With a regal gesture to indicate her willingness for the young commoner to approach, Malvina intoned, "Welcome to Worthington Manor, young lady. We hope you're enjoying the tour."

Cloris didn't know what to do, so she curtsied.

Malvina noticed how petite the girl was; noticed that she was the sort who did her own hair, at home; noticed she was wearing a cloth coat of rather poor quality. *Reynolds, Reynolds, Reynolds.*

She said, "You are going to introduce us, aren't you, Reynolds?"

"Absolutely, M'mah. Cloris, this is my mother. M'mah, this is Cloris. Cloris Schermer."

Malvina's reaction was immediate as if, puppet-like, strings were tugging at her, yanking her into a near corner with her back to her company. She assumed a tight, defensive posture with clenched fists. Reynolds hurried to her side.

"M'mah, what's wrong?"

In a whisper that could be heard throughout the room, Malvina said, "Get her out of my sight, out of my house. Get her out before I strangle the bitch with my bare hands."

Whether or not she meant to be heard other than by Reynolds, Cloris didn't know, but she wasn't deaf. She fled. Reynolds was rooted in place for a moment or two, then he hurried after her.

CHAPTER 7

The County Seat

From in front of Saint Peter's Cathedral at the crest of the hill, the heavily trafficked Main Street sashays downhill in a north-to-south direction past the County Court House and its Annex, then eases past the YMCA and the Episcopal Church, and cuts across a handful of east-to-west thoroughfares before finally reaching the parking lot of the *Lucky Jack Supermarket*. It has cut right through the heart of town, a town that had once been a thriving retail center, but had only taken ten years to sink into near dereliction when the deep coal mines closed in the 1950's.

Main Street has been totally rehabilitated now, thanks to the expansion of the Catholic college, Our Lady of Mercy, whose original buildings occupy an adjoining hill that can be seen over beyond the railroad station. There is a fine brick building for the Theatre Department now and a building for science classrooms and labs named after GrandP'pah Hughes, and a structure with faux marble pillars called the Hall of Justice—the Police Department and the new lockup. There are lots of storefronts freshly painted now, their windows routinely washed. Cafes, lawyers' offices, a CVS and a Rite Aid. Even *Tipson's Posies* has a fresh look, although it never had a very fancy front to begin with, and Old Man Tipson is long dead, and his widow is not up to much anymore.

It was Cloris Schermer who saw to the refurbishment of the flower shop. Finding herself at loose ends after returning to the County after graduating State U, and given her love of flowers, Cloris volunteered to help sweet old Mrs. Tipson—her husband having upped and died, leaving the records of accounts receivable in shoe boxes and leaving his widow a weeping helpless heap—Cloris volunteered to help around the shop with the flowers and accounts. In exchange for learning the business, which she quickly did. She will soon be the proprietor.

Cloris is working there now.

She is standing behind a counter, well toward the back of the shop but facing the door. In front of her are two tall, narrow-necked glass vases filled with flowers—dusky rose, pink, lilac, deep purple. She adds wheat stalks, Baby's Breath, lush leaves. She is wearing a short-sleeved shirtwaist dress under a well-worn, full-length apron, both the apron and the dress a floral green color that match the leaves and stems. No gloves. Cloris loves the way the flowers feel to her hands, the way they smell. Her fingers, like prima ballerinas, can be seen pirouetting among the flowers and greenery.

Reynolds Hughes parked his BMW sedan at the yellow curb in front of the *Big 'n Tall Mens*, confident that no cop would mistake his vehicle and ticket it. He strolled past *WeeGee's Tavern*, wrinkling his nose at the stench of stale beer; he passed the *Wine & Spirits* and approached the front of *Tipson's Posies*. Looked in the large front window and, as expected, saw Cloris Schermer behind a counter toward the back of the shop. She was arranging the flowers in vahses. It appeared as if Old Lady Tipson was not on the premises. *Good.*

Of course, Cloris noticed someone at the window looking in, and of course she recognized him. He was wearing dark brown slacks and designer sunglasses, but no hat. Cloris remembered hearing, maybe from Reynolds himself, that Hughes men never wore hats. Besides, he had on a honey-colored, Italian leather bomber jacket that no other young man in the County could have afforded.

She knew it probably wasn't fair to blame Reynolds for her violent rejection by his mother, but the sight of him in the window had begun to give Cloris stomach cramps.

"If you've come courting," she called to him when the door opened, "Edwina Tipson's not here."

The door was just enough ajar to accommodate

Reynolds' head. He said, "Very funny, Cloris, but may I have a word?"

"Oh boy, yes. The girl who was thrown out of Worthington Manor last night," she said, "definitely has a word for you."

"Seriously, Cloris…"

"I'm warning you, Reynolds, I've been insulted by you and your mother for the last time."

"By me? How did I? I never…"

"Well, alright, not you, but your mother…"

"I agree with you one hundred percent. Couldn't we, maybe, discuss it?"

"Well, I don't see what there is to discuss, but okay, if you must. Don't just stand there. Come in."

But he couldn't come in, Hughes men were sorely affected by the scent of flowers. Like onions to vampires, not an allergy, a revulsion. Since Reynolds could not go into the flower shop, he coaxed her to come out.

"I'll buy you a coffee," he said, thinking of the *Juice 'n Java* across the street.

He was not to be denied. Cloris relented and agreed to take a break. She draped a cardigan over her shoulders, exited the shop—noticing Reynolds' cologne as she passed him, how lovely it was, how expensive it must have been—and dashed across the street. He hustled across to open the door for her, and led her to a two-top in a corner shared by a couple absorbed in their laptops and ear buds. *Perfect privacy.*

Without asking her what she wanted, Reynolds got into the short queue and bought them each a large latte. Returning to the table he noticed the storm warnings were still up. *Too late,* he realized, *should have asked what she wanted.*

Her voice the growl of a she-bear, Cloris said, "Hughes men always get what they want, don't they?"

His only reply was a gesture, a bit more than a shrug but a lot less than a denial.

She thought about spilling her latte on Reynolds' head. Decided not to spoil his fifty-dollar haircut.

Reynolds pried off the lid of his latte, tore open a pink bag of sweetener, careful not to spill any on the table, and added the sweetener to his latte. Next, he took up a swizzle stick and stirred slowly twice to the right, twice to the left, then used a paper napkin to blot the swizzle stick and place it carefully on the table parallel to the napkin.

Cloris watched the entire ritualistic operation, rolling her eyes as her anger mounted. She reached across the table, snatched up the swizzle stick and holding it in front of Reynolds' face, snapped it in half.

Reynolds kept his cool. He said, "Look, I know you're angry, you have every right to be. I came here to see you and apologize. Not for M'mah, I can't apologize for her, she'll have to do that herself..."

Fat chance.

"I can only apologize for myself and, well, I mean, I do."

He paused, unaccustomed to apologizing for anything, and feeling as if he were getting nowhere, treading through molasses.

"I do apologize, sort of, although I don't see how I could have foreseen such a violent reaction from M'mah. And her reaction was not to you but to your name, Schermer. I don't think she has anything against you personally, apparently, it's something between her and your family. Something between the Hugheses and the Schermers. But what? She won't say. I asked and she wouldn't say. Refused to. Have you any idea what's going on, Cloris? I don't."

Reynolds, cluelessness on his face, a mustache of latte on his upper lip.

Cloris couldn't help but smile, couldn't help but climb off his case.

She said, "Hugheses? Is that how you say it? Hugheses?"

"Get serious, Cloris. This is serious."

"I'm sorry, I couldn't help it. I don't know what gives between the Hugheses and the Schermers, but I do know that my mother goes ballistic every time she hears the name, Hughes. The reasons she gives make no sense. They make her sound like a Commie.

Which she isn't. The wealthy this, the wealthy that. Really."

"She does, she goes ballistic?"

Reynolds watched her make a mouth and nod. He put his cup carefully on the table top and slid forward in his chair. He said, "What's to be done, Cloris? This can't go on. Not if we're to…you know, you and me."

She looked at him closely. "What's this, you and me?"

"Come on, Cloris, you know. You and me."

She hadn't thought of them that way, not really, not seriously. But she realized that she had better, in the future.

"Oh," she said, trying to hide her surprise. "*That* you and me. I see. Yes, you and me. Well."

CHAPTER 8

Cloris Does Lunch

The doors of *Chez Stanlí* had opened to horrible reviews. The restaurant critic of the *City Gazette*, while noting its chic décor, suggested that, to quote him:

Dear readers, have drinks, by all means, but the food is not to be eaten.

The Arts critic of The *Post-Examiner* –it doesn't have a dedicated restaurant critic—called the décor French Pretentious and the food Pedestrian Predictable, with capital 'P's.

Cloris wondered what had so infuriated the critics. Was it the background music, the incessant warbling of a woman with a tin ear and halting high school French, poorly imitating Edith Piaf? Was it the topping of the burgers with Roquefort cheese being the only thing French about the food? Or were the critics antagonized by the proprietor himself? Monsieur Stanlí—aka Stanley Greenbaum—was a little man with a goatee, waxed moustache, a black beret and a phony

French accent. Still, Cloris suspected *Chez Stanlí* would provide just the right atmosphere for a reunion with her old college roommate, Meredith Goodlyn.

It was M. Stanlí himself who greeted Cloris at the reservation desk. "*Enchanté, Mlle.*" He bowed over her left hand as if to peck at it, then he made a pretense of noticing the ring set on the third finger. "*'Scusé moi, but Mme* is so young looking…"

Cloris frowned, rolled her eyes. She was led to a 2-top in a perfect position to observe people as they entered the café; at the same time, she was able to admire the décor. The walls were covered with scenes of the 19th century *Moulin Rouge* a la Toulouse Lautrec. The menu covers bore French ballet scenes by the impressionist Edgar Degas. Immediately Cloris was pleased with her choice of *Chez Stanlí* for their reunion, remembering that Meredith had studied high school French and that Meredith enjoyed French wines. At least she used to. She had when they last met three years ago.

Cloris had dressed thoughtfully for the occasion: white cotton slacks, a yellow long-sleeve blouse and matching yellow sandals with a low heel. What Cloris called carefully casual. She knew her old roomie's taste in clothes ran to frumpy in her attempt to hide the fact that she was a little overweight. The Omega Rho's …*Grrr*…blackballed Meredith because they said that Meredith was broad in the beam and flat in the chest. Cloris had to admit her roomie was a bit frumpy, a bit nerdy and, yes, a bit overweight. *So what? She is my friend. Screw the Omega Rho's.*

Cloris and Meredith were roomies for their freshman and sophomore years at Penn State. At the end of those two happy years, however, Meredith announced her intention not to return to Happy Valley the following September. She intended instead to transfer her credits to MIT or better yet, CMU, which was close to her parents' home in Pittsburgh. CMU, according to her, was much less a party place than Happy Valley.

With at least one hundred miles between the two young women, their meetings were few for the remainder of those college years, except for e-mails. After graduation their meetings fell off to zero, the one exception being the get-together three years ago. At that time Cloris was newly married and Meredith was working for Dow Chemical in West Virginia. The passage of time hadn't affected their relationship. Meredith hadn't changed, they were still as close as...

There was a flash of light from the entranceway, it turned out to be the sun high in the noon sky glinting off a woman's garment. But what a woman and what a garment: a high fashion jumpsuit that from a distance appeared to be made from small squares of highly polished leather or perhaps pieces of ebony the size of *Mah Jong* tiles. It was sleeveless, backless and for the most part frontless. The jumpsuit, the platform heels, matching bag, blond hair in a stylish pixie cut and topped off with a black leather motorcyclist's cap—the woman was stunning. She was coming this way. Cloris's jaw dropped when she recognized the stunner as her old roomie.

"Close your mouth, Sweetie," Meredith Goodlyn said, smiling, blue eyes bright with satisfaction at Cloris's reaction. "You're letting the flies in."

A stunned Cloris was glued to her chair. "Is it really you, Mer? My god, you're so, so…"

"Aren't I, though." Meredith was about to air-peck at her college roommate's cheek, but a panicked Cloris halted her.

"Don't bend over," Cloris said. "You'll fall out of the top of that…"

"You mean these," Meredith said, cupping her considerable breasts and giving them a little shake. "Aren't they something? What are you boys gaping at?" She was referring to M. Stanlí and a waiter, both of whom were frozen in place and were indeed gaping.

Meredith laughed, waited for M. Stanlí to hold her chair.

After seating her, the proprietor went off and the server hovered. Meredith said, "I guess I've changed since we last met, haven't I? I've had a makeover. The hair, a personal trainer, contact lenses, new wardrobe, the tits. Cost me practically the entire divorce settlement, but it was worth every penny, don't you think?"

"You're divorced? I didn't even know you were married."

"Yeah. Married and divorced, all in two years. You?"

"Still married, very happily married, actually. Reynolds and I are very happy, really." Cloris wondered why she was so anxious to convince Meredith that she and Reynolds were happy. *Oh well.*

Meredith said, "Well, that's just dandy. Let's order champagne, the very best in the house, okay? We'll drink a toast to both marriage and divorce." They did.

"Tell me about your marriage, Mer."

Meredith shrugged. "What's to tell?"

She met him—him being Herr Broderich Braun—in Vegas. Herr Braun spoke English with a rather romantic German accent. Meredith was in Las Vegas to deliver a paper before the ISOC.

Cloris said, "You gave a paper before The International Olympic Committee?"

"No, silly!"

Meredith meant the International Society of Organic Chemists. Had Cloris forgotten she was an organic chemist? Anyway, Broderich Braun was at the convention to represent the interests of the company he worked for.

"Get this, Cloris. The company he worked for, the company his family happens to be major stockholders of, was Bundren-Braun A.G. You've heard of Bundren-Braun A.G., haven't you? One of the largest pharmaceuticals and chemicals companies in the world?

Anyway, Rick Braun asked Meredith out on a date that started on a Friday afternoon, a wild drunken affair that lasted all weekend, and when she woke up in his bed on Monday morning, she discovered she was *Mrs*. Broderich Braun.

"Happens all the time in Vegas."

"Sounds daring and exciting. Not at all like you, Mer."

While that drunken weekend *was* exciting, or as much of it as Meredith remembered was, the marriage was anything but. Rick Braun was a nice enough guy, but by the time one year had passed, Meredith was bored out of her mind.

"I wanted out," Meredith said. "Turns out Rick did too. He settled a nice sum on me and we split. End of story.

"Enough about me. Tell me, Clo. Is your husband a really good dentist? I need some work." Meredith inserted a finger in her mouth and gurgled, as people do whenever dentistry is mentioned.

"Reynolds is a specialist, a periodontist. He only does gums, Mer. For fillings and such, you need a general dentist."

"Make that an *unmarried* general dentist, please," Meredith said. "Don't you just love it when they're working in your mouth and they're trying to peek down the top of your blouse at the same time? I wear my deepest scoop-neck top and a micro bra to dental appointments. Gives them a thrill." They both laughed.

"But seriously, Clo. How are you getting along with your mother-in-law? Still having problems? Mine was a real pip, a Nazi war criminal. But I was rid of her when I got rid of him. You?"

What was true at their last meeting hadn't changed, Cloris admitted. Malvina Hughes still owned the entire County, and she still tried to make everybody in the County dance to her tune. Especially the daughter-in-law who she had never thought good enough for her son in the first place.

Meredith had heard or read somewhere that the best way to handle a difficult mother-in-law was to have a baby. "Not that I did that, hon. I went the divorce route, but maybe you ought to try the baby thing?"

Staring into her empty champagne flute, Cloris said, "We've been trying. God knows we have. So far, no luck."

"What we need is another glass of champagne. We'll drink a toast to better luck." Meredith looked at the watch on her wrist. "Oh, but, no. I've gotta run. Job interview in half an hour, twelfth floor, Gulf Building. Some other time. We'll get together soon, okay?"

They both stood, embraced. Cloris, her face

close to Meredith's cheek, said, "My god, what are you wearing?"

"Like it? It's my signature scent."

"It's so down and dirty. It smells like…"

"Yeah."

CHAPTER 9

Hands In

T he hostas had shed their blooms and the anemone stalks were standing tall and blooming white. The pepper bushes were heavy with tiny black beads. The viburnum's leaves were on fire and the sedums were blushing pink, but the petunias they had planted in the first week of May were cheerless and withered in this first week of September. They—Cloris Hughes and Bruno Maestromateo—are at their annual chore, for the third year, of ripping out the petunias, spreading a fresh layer of mushroom compost and setting in the chrysanthemum seedlings.

Cloris was the only one of Mattie's customers with whom he had ever worked, nor could he recall any other customer asking to or even hinting at wanting to pitch in with the work. They hired Mattie to do that. He called upon a small crew of young laborers when he needed a hand with the heavy stuff, but whenever possible he preferred being alone with his plants. Mattie loved his work, but he had to admit he especially loved sharing the work with this woman, Missus Hughes, who so loved it.

There was Mattie in Oshkosh overalls and peaked cap, spreading with a rake and there next to him was Cloris, dressed in jeans and a sweatshirt, kneeling on a garden stool with trowel in hand. They were working silently and steadily until Cloris paused to watch him.

Mattie was trying to spread compost evenly atop the flowerbed. He shook his head in dissatisfaction, threw down the rake, got down with a groan on all fours and began raking the compost with his fingers. *That was better*. Cloris, admiring his work, said, "Mattie, I think I'm in love."

Startled, Mattie said, "With me? I'm too old for you."

"I don't mean in a romantic way, exactly. I…"

"'At's a good thing," he said. "I'm married thirty-five year. My wife's a jealous woman and her brother is a 'made' guy. I wouldn't survive a year." They both laughed.

Cloris loved that the old man's hands were always dirty, that there was always dirt under his finger nails. She said, "Reynolds, my husband, washes his hands forty or fifty times a day. His hands are always clean." She wasn't sure that was a good thing. Mattie didn't think so.

They returned to the work.

* * *

At the same time as the chrysanthemums were being set into compost, no more than five miles away in a once derelict downtown building that had previously been dedicated to the practice of business law and estates and had been converted—while still preserving as much of the dark mahogany woodwork as was humanly possible—converted to the practice of periodontal dentistry, Reynolds Hughes D.M.D. was thoroughly, meticulously washing his hands.

Dr. Hughes had just completed a gingivectomy followed by scaling and curettage of the maxillary right dentition of Mrs. Edna Barnstable. The surgical mask now down off his patrician's face, latex gloves off his hands, Reynolds Hughes took in a deep breath and held it and with his eyes closed, reviewed in his mind each move he had made with his hands. Satisfaction spread across his face. He was pleased with the results of his work, pleased with the speed with which it had been accomplished. Pleased with himself. This mental reenactment—was it confidence, was it arrogance?—was observed by the other people who happened to be present in the operatory:

1) a young assistant, a recent high school graduate who was newly hired, moving slowly and with great deliberation so as not to make mistakes with what she had just been taught: the collection of all soiled paper goods and gauze and dividing them into categories for disposal, either ordinary trash or hazardous waste.

2) the office manager Millie Tagliafaro, a heavy set, gray haired black woman of an age—meaning no one in the office knew her age, not even the doctor. Mrs. Tagliafaro stood by the door, keeping a mother hen's eye on the new hire.

3) Lorann Petrillo, surgical assistant, attractive brunette in her early thirties. She was packing the surgical site in the patient's mouth with a putty-like substance with analgesic qualities. Once this post-op mission was accomplished, Lorann helped the patient off with the surgical drape and helped her to tidy up.

4) the patient herself, Mrs. Edna Barnstable, a woman of fifty years, more or less, who was anxious for the procedure to be concluded and anxious to be out of the operatory, yet she followed Dr. Hughes' every movement with admiring eyes.

Without uttering a word but by pointing a finger here and there, Mrs. T indicated a few contaminated items that had been missed, then a flutter of her wrist sent the young assistant scurrying with her burdens to the sterilization room.

Mrs. T's father had been with the U.S. Marines; it was no coincidence that his eldest child, Mrs. T, had the manner and temperament of a drill sergeant. She had been Dr. Hughes' very first hire, when the office was still just an architect's blueprint. She trained the staff and organized the routines of the office, deferring, of course, to Dr. Hughes on matters of aesthetic taste and surgical protocols. She treated the staff with respect, while suffering no fools and no foolishness, and the staff accepted her leadership without apparent resentment. Consequently, the office of Reynolds Hughes DMD was an exemplar of efficiency.

Mrs. T was the office's sergeant major. While Mrs. T would never dream of saluting Dr. Hughes or addressing him as sir, he was the five-star general. He was only slightly more than six feet tall but everyone thought him to be taller because his posture was so military; he always seemed to be standing at attention.

Anyone familiar with Dr. Hughes and his background might question the veracity of the military analogy, since neither he nor any member of the Worthington County Hughes clan, to the best of their knowledge, had ever served in the military. For Reynolds, an athletic pose on the cover of *Tennis Monthly* would be a better fit than the military. With his tall, broad-shouldered build, he would look splendid wearing white tennis shorts and a loose, short-sleeved top with a white cable knit sweater draped over his shoulders, the sleeves tied in front.

Healthy, wealthy and fit, that was Reynolds Hughes. Here in the office he was wearing his usual uniform: a white poplin doctor's coat over navy trousers, matching navy tie and a pale blue silk shirt.

The Hugheses owned the legal rights to every lump of coal in Worthington County, but not one of them had ever dug a lump out of the ground. As far as Reynolds knew, no Hughes had ever labored with his hands, except to rake in wealth by the fistful. They were patricians. Had they existed in ancient times, they would have been members of the Roman Senate, togas, sandaled feet and all.

And Reynolds was their pride and joy; he was their legacy. He was their legacy at Groton, their legacy at Princeton, their legacy at B. Reynolds Hughes & Son, Inc. Reynolds' father, B. Reynolds Hughes II, and his grandfather, B. Reynolds Hughes I, were mildly amused when the teenage Reynolds dropped the B. from his signature; they were no longer amused when he dropped the III; they were incensed when he announced that he was no longer interested in joining the family firm, that he intended instead to work with his hands in, of all places, people's mouths. But they got over it.

Dr. Reynolds Hughes, scion of the wealthy and powerful Hughes clan, had inherited their wealth, their intelligence, their ambition, the handsome patrician's dignity and more than a little of the arrogance of the Hughes men, and the steadfastness—call it stubbornness, if you must—of the Hughes women, but he had a quality that he hadn't inherited from either of them—charm. An all-pervasive charm that Reynolds wore like a second skin, that engulfed him and radiated from him as an aura.

Like metals to a magnet, his charm drew people to him, and as they were drawn to him, they were nodding, yes. Mother, Father and Grandfather Hughes, having been exposed—smiled at, coaxed, cajoled— found his charm to be as catching as a potent virus to which they had no immunity and no resistance. So, he got his way.

He has completed the washing of the hands and is about to confer with Mrs. T as to the patients he is to see to complete his morning's work.

Mrs. T consulted her note pad. She said, "All three hygienists have patients in their chairs. You'll have those exams to complete when the hygienists are done."

Dr. Hughes nodded. "That will take me up to lunch time, I hope?"

"It does." She frowned. "According to my notes, you have a luncheon engagement at noon." She looked at him. "You didn't say with whom."

"I didn't, did I."

"No, you didn't, and best I don't know. You have two implants at two o'clock. Mr. Mickelson."

"Could we change that to three o'clock? I might need…more time."

"Try not to… need more time, alright? One more thing, a comment on your, shall I say relationship? With Lorann. If you don't mind. I'd like, I'd prefer, to see a little more distance between you and her in the future. A little less contact with her on your part, if you catch my meaning. I'd not like another…"

"Say no more, dear Mrs. T, I understand perfectly and I concur." He raised his hands in a gesture of surrender. "My conduct with Lorann will be pristine and exemplary."

He already has another fish on the hook, Mrs. T thought.

Reynolds walked off toward his private sanctum, admiring as he went the mahogany wainscoting, colonnades and moldings throughout the office that he had insisted be restored.

Such magnificent workmanship, genius of me to demand...

CHAPTER 10

Dinner at Townie's

Seven p.m. at the dusky end of a blue-white diamond of a July day. Reynolds Hughes eased his red BMW to the curb in front of *Posies* just as Cloris Schermer engaged the bolt to secure the front door. She waited by the car's passenger door, as he insisted she do, waiting for Reynolds to come around and open it for her. She had a powerful dislike for his mother, but Cloris gave her credit—Malvina Hughes had raised Reynolds to be a gentleman. Old fashioned, yes, but it tickled Cloris where she lived to be in the hands of a gentleman.

When she was seated and he was comfortably ensconced behind the wheel, Reynolds drew in a deep breath through his patrician's prominent nose; like all Hughes men, he disliked what to him was the funereal smell of flowers. But on her it wasn't so unpleasant, and he told her so. She explained that one of the local gladiola farmers had delivered a truckload that morning, so she was elbow-deep in gladiolas all day.

"Well, you smell splendid," he said, leaning close, then he kissed her on the mouth. Cloris found it hard to sit still.

"What would you like to do tonight, Clo? You haven't eaten, have you?"

She didn't know what she wanted to do, not much, since she had been working all day and was tired. But no, she hadn't eaten. She said, "Maybe we could grab a burger somewhere?"

He said, "Sometimes I think you've forgotten you're not in high school any more. You talk just like a teenager." He imitated her: "Maybe we could grab a burger somewhere." They both laughed. Then he said, "Maybe we could go to the drive-in theatre and not watch the movie."

They looked at each other seriously, both thinking it a wonderful idea and both regretting the County's only drive-in theatre had closed.

"But you're right about me," she said. "I wouldn't mind being back in high school, I wouldn't mind being a teenager forever. Teen years are pretty much care free. At least mine were." *Well yes,* she thought, *except for my having lost my father and having a wicked witch of the West for a mother*.

"Not for me, they weren't," Reynolds said, which made her wonder what a manor-borne type, silver spoon and all, could possibly have disliked about his teen years. He said, "Private schools are all business, and I mean serious business, at least the ones I was forced to attend were. The schools my P'pah and GrandP'pah had attended. Me, the legacy. Nose to the grindstone. Chapel every morning. Hit the books. Lights out at 9:30."

"Poor boy," she said, unable to get sympathy into her voice. "I guess you were glad to come back home on holidays."

"Well…" He slipped the car into Drive and headed out of the downtown without finishing the sentence.

Cloris swiveled around in her seat as far as the seat belt permitted so she could face him. She loved to watch him drive. Reynolds Hughes handled the BMW with easy confidence, in complete control, as if man and machine were of one certain mind. She wanted to touch him, she wanted to rest her nose against the nape of his neck and breathe him in; she was hungry, she wanted to eat him up.

Not that they had far to go. Two lefts at the intersection at the bottom of Main Street hill and they had arrived at *Townie's*, a sports bar that served arguably the best burgers in the County, and if a patron wasn't interested in the games on TV, it was a beautiful warm night with a waning moon for occupying one of the round tables on the patio.

They ordered blue cheese burgers, a glass of red wine for her and a Belgian beer that he fancied. If she were out with any other guy—how long had it been since she was out with any other guy?—being as tired as she was after working in the shop all day, she would have been careful to avoid anything alcoholic. Better safe than sorry, but she trusted Reynolds.

He went into the bar to visit the restroom; she sipped her wine and waited impatiently for his return. It had turned dark and the night was very still; the candle the waitress had placed on their table burned steadily and straight; Cloris found herself enveloped in a very dreamy glow.

Returning to the patio, Reynolds was seen framed in the doorway with the bar's light behind him. He was dressed for the evening as he usually was, expensively, tieless but neatly tieless: shirt, slacks, sports jacket, as if he had just stepped off the cover of *GQ*. Tall, beautiful and confident, as if the world were his. Cloris saw that and realized then—as if she hadn't before—that she too was his.

Reseated next to her, Reynolds found a look on her face that he hadn't seen before but suspected he was the cause of. He said, "I did something wrong, didn't I? I didn't mean to, I swear. Whatever it was."

She said, "I need to ask you something." He wondered if she were teasing him again. "No, seriously. Do you really try, I mean, do you work at looking great all the time? Or does it come easy when you have more money than God? No insult intended, I really need to know."

"Really, Cloris, I..."

"And another thing, while I'm asking. I'm way out of your league, B. Reynolds Hughes the Third.

Why Cloris Schermer from the 'other side' of town? Why me?"

He looked perplexed, but only for a minute. He said, "Well, if we're being honest with each other..." She agreed that they were. "But I'm curious why you're asking now. Did I do or say something... "She shook her head. "Then why now?"

She said, "Not why *now*. Why later. *Now* we're being honest with each other. You first, okay?"

Reynolds shrugged. "Okay. Well, first, we, the Hughes family, we don't have more money than God. However, we do have a lot. That's nothing to be ashamed of, if you ask me. I'm not ashamed of it, I'm proud of it. Second, the way I dress. The way I dress is the way I've always dressed. I enjoy clothes and I'm fortunate that I'm able to have expensive things. Sue me, but I don't know any other way. As for your being from the other side of town, that's never mattered to me. The truth is, I've always been attracted to you, Cloris, ever since we were kids. Really attracted. Granted, we never went to the same schools..."

"That's the understatement of all understatements."

"Yes, but I always came home hoping to get a glimpse of you, often contriving, really contriving to *accidentally* run into you."

"But why?"

"I haven't *said* why because I don't *know* why.

Does anyone ever know why they're attracted to some-body? They just are. Haven't you heard of people falling in love, Cloris?"

She picked up the remaining half of her burger and took a bite; while chewing she weighed in her mind the risk of being honest with him. Bleu cheese sauce oozed out and dripped onto the table in front of her. Everything to lose, nothing in particular to gain by honesty, but she couldn't resist.

"Yes, I've heard of people falling in love and, since we're being perfectly honest, I think I've fallen in love with you. In fact, I *know* I have."

"Good," Reynolds said. He tapped a finger into Cloris's run-away bleu cheese sauce and dabbed it onto the tip of her nose. "That puts us in the same boat." Then he proceeded to lick it off.

Much later, Reynolds drove back up Main Street and around to Cloris's parking spot in the alley be-hind *Posies*. They hugged and kissed and reluctantly said their good nights. It was almost morning. They went their separate ways, he to Worthington Manor, she to the house on the 'other side' where she lived with her mother. Harrison Avenue wasn't far, and a good thing it wasn't, for Cloris was lost behind the wheel. Already she missed his arms around her. His sudden absence made her feel as if she were wilting, like a flower desperate for water.

Cloris removed her shoes and carried them into the house, hoping her mother was asleep, hoping to avoid another confrontation. No such luck.

Katherine Schermer staggered over her flip-flop slippers as she tried to rise too quickly from the living room sofa. Her ratty robe had come undone to reveal a thin cotton gown that hadn't seen an iron, and Cloris noticed her mother's ragged mop of gray hair hadn't been brushed.

Katherine said, "Well, lookit who's here, the prodigal daughter. I was expecting you for supper, had to throw it out. I hope you ate something somewhere." She waited for Cloris to answer, but Cloris didn't. "Well, did ya? Eat something, I mean? Somewhere? I had to throw out a perfectly good dinner, least I deserve is an answer."

"I don't think you do," Cloris replied. "We've discussed this before. I'm not beholden to you for a report of my every move. Those days are long gone."

"They are, I know they are, but I still worry, don't I? You're still my daughter and when I see you're doing something wrong, making a terrible mistake, I feel responsible..."

"What terrible mistake am I making this time? And why are you responsible?"

"Why, you're going out with... You know perfectly well, you're seeing that Hughes boy."

"He's not a boy, mother. He's a grown man, a very

nice man." She thought, *A very, very, nice man, and very grown.* "You keep accusing me of doing something wrong, but why is it wrong to see Reynolds Hughes? You refuse to elaborate."

To Cloris's surprise, Katherine Schermer opened her mouth as if to reply, but no sound came out of her throat. Even in the dim light of the living room at that early hour, Cloris could see her mother's color heighten, but no sound came out of her mouth.

Mother must have a good reason for holding her tongue, Cloris thought, *at least she thinks it's a good reason. But good or bad, whatever it is beats me. Or was it the vodka?* Sure enough. Leaning close to place a reluctant peck on her mother's cheek, she was sure she smelled vodka.

Suddenly exhausted and desperate for a few hours' sleep before she next had to open *Posies*, Cloris said, "Nothing more to say, mother? Then, good night."

Off she went to bed. It had been a hell of a day.

CHAPTER 11

The Coach *and* Eight

Old Route 30 wanders through the Laurel Highlands foothills seemingly without aim or ambition. The *Coach and Eight Inn & Tavern* huddles down on a wide point in that old road, just before it begins its struggling climb mountain-ward. The *Inn and Tavern's* present owner claims it was made over from the stagecoach way-station of a bygone era. Maybe. No one knows or cares.

The inn rooms upstairs are only man-clean, the local women say, and the restaurant fare is fair, but the main room has a great fireplace, great in size and depth—a man could stand erect in it—a great log fire to sit by in early November with a mug of hot, spicy cider in your fist and the spectacle still in your memory of rust-gold leaves that you passed on the way here. Reynolds Hughes and Cloris Schermer, not yet sure about the depth of their relationship, are doing just that.

The main tavern room smells of cinnamon and nutmeg and candle wax and log fires. Heavy oaken tables and oaken chairs are cracked and worn by time and the pants of two centuries of weary travelers. Coarse stone floor in front of the fireplace, rough-hewn board floors elsewhere. Sparks from the fireplace seem to leap and dance on the lacquered pine boards that panel the walls, candlelight from chandeliers made from iron wagon wheels. Everything is old, worn, authentic and wonderful on a cold, clear November night.

The radio is set very low on an FM classical station; there are few patrons, this being a weeknight, and the ambient conversation is a murmur.

Because Reynolds was tall, Cloris knew she could wear her new boots with lots of heel that she picked up on sale at *Payless*—Did they look cheap? She hoped they didn't look cheap. She was wearing soft black trousers and a black cashmere sweater that was very much in a holiday mood and also made the most of her figure. She noticed Reynolds' eyes were drawn to the sweater. She doubted that had anything to do with the red sequins.

She said, "See something you like, Reynolds?" Watched him blush. She had meant to embarrass him, but then she was sorry she had succeeded.

She said, "You look good too. What does M'mah think you're up to tonight?"

"I wish you wouldn't make fun of me that way."

He wished, but it was no use and he knew it. He shrugged. "She thinks I'm at the club." He said *the club* as if it were capitalized. "It's Men's Monte Carlo Night to raise money for charity. No ties allowed."

"I wondered. I've rarely seen you without a tie. But I love the jacket. You should be smoking a pipe."

He thanked her, saying he loved it too. Camel's hair was his favorite, and he especially loved the casual feel of the elbow patches. A bit dressy for a Monte Carlo Night, he admitted, but M'mah was bound to conclude that no tie meant a men's event at the club.

"You lied to your mother? Naughty boy."

"No, I would never lie to M'mah. When she jumped to the wrong conclusion, I failed to correct her. A big difference."

"Yes, indeed. Well, I'm no better," Cloris confessed. "I told my mother I was going to the Palace Theatre to see my favorite Bluegrass band. I even invited her to come along. Said I'd buy her a ticket at the door."

"That was risky, that could've backfired."

"Not really, she hates Bluegrass music."

They both laughed at that, although Cloris guessed Reynolds agreed with her mother about hating Bluegrass music.

They sipped at their cider mugs and snuggled a little closer to the fire and to each other. Of course, they recognized themselves for what they were, cowards. They had been seeing each other for weeks, like teenagers telling lies to avoid confrontations with their mothers. Could they continue on that course? Cloris thought not, Reynolds didn't say.

She said, "You can't keep on lying to your mother and neither can I. You're too well-known in the County; people talk, M'mah will find…"

"Cloris, I wish you wouldn't…"

"I'm sorry. *Your mother* will find out, so will mine."

"Maybe so, still I hate the thought of telling her I'm dating Cloris Schermer, she'll have a stroke. I'm surprised she didn't have one last time."

That gave Cloris pause. She concluded that Reynolds would procrastinate rather than confront his mother, if he could, if she let him. The time had come to lay it on the line. She took a swallow of her cider, then took a deep breath and plunged in.

"You know, Reynolds," she said, "From the first moment when you started talking about you and me as if you and me was an entity that really existed, that it was an actual thing, I wondered, were you really serious about me, or was what you had in mind for me a trip to the *Short Stay Motel*? Well, I'm still wondering. Which is it, Reynolds? You and me for real, or the *Short Stay Motel*?"

"Well, Cloris, I'm thinking," he said, "why can't it be both? I was hoping…"

He smiled, but she saw he was serious. She cozied even closer to him and thought, *Wouldn't it be wonderful if at this moment the fire were to melt the two of us into one.*

* * *

It was now close to midnight and very dark along that old road, but further up the mountain was a motel called simply, Motel. Not a Motel 6 or Holiday Inn, a poorly lighted and poorly kept place. In slightly smaller letters, the sign read: SHORT STAY $24.95.

Eight units could be seen, four doors and four picture windows with drapes fully drawn on each side of an office. A crack of dim blue light showed from a fluorescent bulb where the warped office door failed to meet the jamb perfectly. Despite the darkness, finding the place was no challenge for Reynolds; he pulled his BMW sedan into the motel parking lot as if he knew where he was going, as if he had been there before. As if he were in a hurry.

There were vehicles parked in front of two of the units, and those two showed a little light where the drapes failed to meet perfectly. The other units showed dark.

Still in the BMW, Reynolds and Cloris were in each other's arms, hugging, kissing, their hands all over each other.

Once having come up for air Cloris said, "This isn't easy in a car with bucket seats."

"Don't forget this damn gearshift lever, I know I never will."

Reynolds' urgency was as apparent to Cloris as her own. She urged him to hurry inside and register. She said, "You'd better ask for that unit way down at the end. I'm going to make some noise tonight."

"You're not a virgin, are you?"

"After four years in Happy Valley, are you kidding?"

Reynolds reluctantly pulled away from her and exited the car. Half way to the office, seeming to change his mind about something, he returned to the car. Cloris rolled down the window.

She said, "What?"

"I'm going to pay for the entire night. I want to make love to you, and I want to really sleep with you, too." He waited for a reply; he didn't have long to wait.

Cloris said, "Okay, but you'd better hurry or I'm liable to start without you."

Reynolds did hurry.

* * *

Then it was morning.

Where did the night go? Time has flown by for Reynolds and Cloris. They have come down from the mountain, and they are once again in town. In a few minutes Cloris will have to cross Main Street to open the flower shop—Edwina Tipson being incapable of anything much before noon. Her arthritis, you know—but for the moment Cloris and Reynolds are huddled together over their morning coffees at a two-top in the *Juice 'n Java*. The heady smell of roasting beans seems to thicken the air, adding body to their reveries.

They are no longer just friends. They are sitting too close together, their knees intertwined, to be just friends. Their hands find too many excuses to reach out and caress each other, his wrist, the crook of her elbow, her hair. Their eyes linger on each other for too many extra beats. They lean too closely toward each other when they speak, their heads nearly touching.

Cloris came out of her reverie to say, "You have to admit, that motel is a pretty disgusting place."

Reynolds said, "It's a wonderful place."

"Isn't it."

In and out of her dream, sipping her coffee. She asked, "Is it Thursday? We're open till seven o'clock."

He smiled. "You?"

A mock-slap on his wrist. "*Posies*, you letch."

He offered to come by at seven and take her to dinner. She thought it best that she go right home at seven and face her mother.

She said, "Have it out with her once and for all. Let her talk me out of you, if she can. Which I doubt."

He took her hand.

He said, "You're braver than me. I'm sitting here trying to invent an excuse not to face M'mah right now. Not this morning." He shuddered.

"If you think of a way out, let me know."

He said, after a moment's pause, "I have."

"We're not going back to that disgusting motel."

"No, I was thinking we could run away, get married. Then you and I would be a *fait accompli*."

"If that's a proposal…"

"Well… I was thinking we could elope, but this is the real world, not a dream. We have to postpone that idea. See, I'm due back at Tufts in a few days. There's still half of a semester left before I finish my research and defend my findings. With that behind me, I'll be a Board-Certified Periodontist. Doesn't that sound great?"

To Cloris it did sound great, but it did not sound like a profession for a Hughes man. She doubted that it sounded great to Reynolds' M'mah.

She said, "So it's back to Boston."

"Certainly. You needn't worry, though. I'll be back here as soon as I'm finished. I intend to practice here, you know."

"Of course."

"As soon as I'm back, I have to design an office and supervise its construction. Here in the downtown area, I expect. I have my eye on the old Hamilton Law Building on Maple Avenue."

"The one with the pillars?"

"The very one. Of course, the entire interior will have to be re-done."

"Of course."

"And there's staff to be hired and trained…"

Cloris said, "Reynolds, we'll need a place to live. We'll have to find a place of our own. If you think I'll live with your M'mah, you've got another thing coming. I'll never set foot in Worthington Manor again."

"No, not Worthington Manor. I promise, we'll look for a place of our own as soon as I get back. But you see, there's a lot on my plate besides…"

"Besides us, I get it and I'm okay with it. In fact, it's just as well because, just so you'll know, Schermer women don't elope. I know Hughes men don't wear hats and Hughes men can't stand the smell of flowers. You've told me that. Well, I'm telling you, Schermer women don't elope."

"Don't get upset, Cloris. I didn't mean to…"

"I'm not upset, I'm only saying, we Schermer women insist on a nice diamond ring on our finger and we insist on wearing a white gown with a train and veil, and we insist on a nice ceremony with clergy and family present. We don't elope."

Reynolds, trying to suppress a grin, said, "All

you Schermer women? Who are all those Schermer women? And, where are they?"

Cloris tapped herself on the chest. "For starters, there's me, and I'm right here."

CHAPTER 12

Bingo Night

In Hecla—a village about fifteen miles northeast of the County seat—Wednesday night is bingo night, come hell or high water, fifty-two weeks a year at the Baptist church on Third Street. Katherine Schermer was determined not to miss a single one. Not that she gave a damn about bingo; in her mind no more boring a game had ever been invented. And as for Baptists, well, she could take most of them or leave them. Along with the Methodists and the Catholics. But someone she owed *did* care for them—Shepherdess SaraBeulah Strawberry.

Shepherdess Strawberry—in Hecla they used to call her that and they still do to this day. Because Strawberry was her Christian name, and since she was not an officially ordained minister, or anything else official for that matter, they couldn't very well call her Pastor Strawberry or Reverend Strawberry. But what she did, she shepherded the Hecla Baptist flock for more than thirty years, a flock too poor to be able to afford to pay a truly ordained person.

Among other things that happened in that thirty-year time, a young woman by the name of Katherine Schermer got herself into trouble, as much trouble as a young woman could get herself into in those days. Having come in contact with that young woman in trouble, SaraBeulah Strawberry had advised Katherine, guided her and even sheltered her when Katherine's own parents saw fit not to.

So now in her 90's, immensely obese and suffering from diabetes and a mild case of cognitive collapse, Shepherdess Strawberry was in need, and Katherine Schermer felt obliged. Each Wednesday evening Katherine drove the Shepherdess from the County Home, where she now resided, to the Baptist Church in Hecla for bingo, which she dearly loved. Katherine helped her cover the numbers on her bingo card, helped the half ton of her into the stalls of the ladies' restroom, which was frequently necessary, and at the end of the evening saw her back into the loving hands of the caregivers at the County Home. It wasn't charity. Katherine didn't think she believed in charity. It was owed, and Katherine Schermer always paid her debts.

The Schermers, mother and daughter, lived in a small bungalow, well kept up but giving in little by little to time and gravity and the fact that it had not been well built in the first place, on Harrison Avenue in a crowded neighborhood at the North end of town. The end of town people referred to as 'the other end,' on the flat land near the railroad station.

Cloris had lived there her entire life, except when she was dorming it in Happy Valley; Katherine had lived there since the house was deeded to her twenty-five years ago.

Now leaving her friend the Shepherdess with the caregivers, Katherine drove home and parked her rust bucket of a Dodge Dart in the driveway beside the house. She saw that Cloris had not yet returned from the bluegrass concert at the Palace Theatre. Once inside, Katherine removed her dress, an old blue thing with white polka dots that reeked of cigarette smoke after each bingo night—it was a wonder to her, how so many bingo players were smokers. She draped the dress on a wire hanger and hung it to air out on the back porch from a hook she had screwed into a wooden roof support. That done, she wrapped herself in a ratty old robe, poured three fingers of vodka into a jelly glass and settled in with it to watch late night TV.

Later, when Johnny Carson had finished his monologue, had swung his arms as if he were whacking a golf ball, and had chatted with a few of his guests, it was nearly midnight and still there was no sign of Cloris. Katherine made discreet telephone inquiries of friends who worked nights at the police station, one who mopped the floors and another who acted as night dispatcher. Katherine did not locate her daughter, but she learned from the dispatcher that no, there had not been a serious traffic tie up on Otterman Street after the bluegrass concert, primarily because there had *been* no Bluegrass concert; not at the Palace Theatre and not anywhere else that night. So, Cloris had lied.

Nothing like a little vodka, Katherine thought, to take the edge off.

She knew there was something not quite right about her relationship with her daughter, her only daughter, Cloris. A woman of twenty-five years who found it necessary to lie to her mother. To her only mother. Without any reason, definitely without any reason at all for doing so. Acting like a spoiled child, a silly little girl.

It was damn funny, a daughter of hers acting like a rebellious teenager. Who for some reason, for spite maybe, was doing the exact opposite of what she had been advised to do. Was doing the exact thing her mother had advised her not to do. It was a shock for Katherine when, pouring a second three fingers of vodka into the jelly glass, she realized that her daughter, her Cloris, was doing the exact thing she herself had done at Cloris's age, and that Cloris was bound to end up in the same sort of trouble as she had found herself. In. Disaster was pending, sure as shit.

It was hardly sunlight that streamed through the windows to waken Katherine that morning, more like the kind of light, if light was rightfully what you would call it, that oozed from a totally overcast sky, typical of this time of year in that place. It was a blue-gray liquid, but just the same it was enough to rouse her from a troubled, vodka-besotted sleep.

What was left of the morning was spent, in part, on the couch trying not to move and trying to quiet the conga drum pounding in her head. The rest was spent on the back porch, still with only a robe over her under things, dragging in chests full of the biting November air. That air was also the color of blue-gray liquid—like vodka, she thought, like hair of the dog—and not too good to breathe, if what the Clean Air people said about it was true. But Katherine thought it stood a better chance against the hangover than two *Alka-Seltzer*.

Cloris had still not returned, but Katherine no longer concerned herself with locating her daughter. She had a pretty good idea where she had been earlier and who she had been with. She also knew for certain where she was now. She knew Cloris would have opened the flower shop at ten—Edwina Tipson, poor dear, couldn't handle mornings—and wouldn't be home until after closing the shop at seven.

Katherine spent half the afternoon scrounging around in the attic of the house searching for her high school class yearbook, and she spent the remainder of the afternoon peering into the bathroom mirror, looking for the girl she had once been, the beautiful young girl in the photo in that yearbook. She also rehearsed what, after all this time, she knew she needed to tell Cloris, what she had steadfastly refused to tell her in the past.

Katherine sponged dust off the high school yearbook with dampened toilet paper, the dust being proof that it was unlikely that her daughter had ever seen it.

When I do show it to her, Cloris may not believe it. She may not believe that beautiful girl is me. She sees me now and won't believe I was ever beautiful, but I was. Once I was young and I was beautiful, and he adored me.

Katherine took a mouthful of water from the tap, using cupped hands instead of a glass; she immediately spat it into the sink bowl and gazed into the mirror. She saw no broad youthful smile. Now her smile was dull, blunted, worn down. She ran her fingers through hair that was as coarse as a *Brillo* pad. Her eyebrows were thin as sick caterpillars and as much like *Brillo* as her hair. Below the brows, her eyes looked unpleasantly small and sunken and clouded with disappointment. There were deep frown grooves at the corners of her mouth.

Cloris will never believe it when I tell her that he loved me and wanted to marry me. My Brock. The bastard. But who could blame her? Who could see me now and believe it? But yearbook photos don't lie and there I am.

Funny. Every damn day, every damn one, you scrub your teeth, brush your hair, put on your face. You step in front of a bathroom mirror—EEK!—you want to swing around and grab a hold of whoever had snuck up behind you, grab that hag whose face is reflected in the mirror instead of yours.

He adored me. I have to tell her now, should have years ago. Wanted to marry me, Brock did. Run away, get married by a JP in West Virginia, then it would be too late for his father to stop it. What a bastard. B. effing Reynolds effing Hughes Senior. Wanted Brock to marry the Lumber King, Malvin S. Strickland. Haha. Not him, his daughter. The Lumber King's daughter. Malvina. Whoo boy, ugly Malvina.

Katherine used her arms to prop her unsteady self against the sink bowl and continued muttering at the mirror.

This Hughes boy of yours, this Reynolds Hughes, he must be tall and handsome like his father was then, tall and handsome and smart. Oh, yes, he was very smart. But weak, so very weak, too weak to stand up to his evil effing bastard of a father. Left me in the lurch, Brock did, got me in trouble and left me for the Lumber King's daughter, ugly effing Malvina.

That evening as the clock struck seven, after locking the front door of the flower shop, Cloris exited by the back door into the alley where she had parked her car. Immediately after opening the shop that morning, she had changed into the loden-green dress with the *Posies* logo and the comfortable flats she always wore at work. Now walking to her car, she carried her new black *Payless* boots and she had her evening clothes slung over her arm. Glad she had parked out back where she was unlikely to encounter anyone. For goodness sake, this was the 20th century. Nobody was scandalized by anything anymore. Still she couldn't help feeling a little bit sleazy. She had showered at the *Short Stay Motel*, but she imagined she could still smell Reynolds and their love making on herself. Once in the car, she breathed a sigh of relief.

The reliable VW Beetle started right up, Thank God, and she headed for home.

Cloris pulled in and parked behind her mother's old Dart. Entering the front door, she tried to act the casual innocent, hoping not to look like a guilty party as she went about her usual business. She hoped to display some brass in the face of her mother's expected bullying with her usually sour face, the old witch. Cloris could imagine her mother barring her way with arms folded across her chest in an insistent, upright pose. The indignant moral guardian.

Instead she found her mother sprawled drunkenly on the couch, snoring, mumbling and choking as if she were suffering apnea. A nearly empty vodka bottle and jelly glass were on the end table by her mother's outstretched arm, and an old high school yearbook had tumbled from her lap onto the floor.

Sleeping beauty, Cloris thought, rolling her eyes. She felt neither disappointment nor relief. A confrontation with her mother was inevitable, and she was anxious to have done with it, but it would not be tonight. No, not tonight.

She thought about another shower but, starting to pull the loden work dress over her head, she changed her mind. She still smelled Reynolds on herself and had no desire to wash it off.

Chapter 13

Family Saga

There have always been three commissioners—two of the majority political party and one of the minority—entrusted by the electorate with the responsibility for managing the County, but for as long as anyone cared to remember there has been an ex-officio commissioner, a non-elected person without portfolio whose power originated not with the people but with the fact that she was the widow of the County's richest, most powerful man and was also the daughter of the County's second richest man, the—also deceased—Lumber King. That ex-officio commissioner was, of course, Malvina Hughes. She singlehandedly wielded enough power to determine the direction of the County's affairs, either forward or in reverse.

Those inclined to disbelieve that a woman could exercise so much power should check with the members of the Daughters of the American Revolution or the Ladies Episcopal Church League or the YWCA.

Or ask her colleagues on the boards of directors of Minutemen's National Bank or the County Symphony Orchestra or the Art Museum or the Salvation Army. They should ask the President Judge of Common Pleas Court, or Hizzonor the Mayor, the Fire Chief or, for that matter, the Little Sisters of the Poor.

Malvina was a powerhouse. She could push harder than a bulldozer and cut ground out from under someone's feet faster and quicker than a back hoe. She was brash, bullish, determined, undeterred and unrelenting; she suffered a serious case of never-take-no-for-an-answer-itis.

Malvina had always been taller than the other girls at the private schools in which she was enrolled, and tall is a handy trait to possess if you detest having to look up to other people, which she did. She was built large and strong and could be tough when toughness was called for, which made the school girl Malvina an excellent field hockey player and made the adult Malvina an excellent intimidator. But she did have a weakness when it came to her son: she could try to control him and she sometimes did, but only when it suited him. He being as stubborn as his deceased father, and as indomitable as Malvina herself. She could deny Reynolds nothing.

It had to be said for Malvina, she was very honest with herself. She knew she was nothing to look at, and anyone who ever saw her was inclined to agree. Still, as they used to say in the boardroom of Minutemen's National Bank: Money is no less beautiful for being green.

That morning, after unabashedly kissing Cloris goodbye in front of *Tipson's Posies* and watching her disappear inside, Reynolds retrieved his BMW, which he had parked at a yellow curb in front of the *Juice 'n Java*—knowing the County cops wouldn't dare ticket it, which proved correct.

He drove slowly north through town on Main Street and tooled along State Road No. 66. A light rain began to spatter against the windshield. After a few miles he turned onto the property of Worthington Manor. When he pulled into the garage that adjoined the Manor, he saw that the limousine's usual parking slot was empty. Knowing his busybody of a mother, he was not surprised. No, not surprised, but he was a little disappointed and a little relieved at the same time. That meant that his mother and Wilps were not in residence.

The Wilpses, Calvin and Viora, had been in the employ of the Hughes family for three decades: Viora—As a boy Reynolds respectfully called Viora Mrs. Wilps and he still did—as both cook and housekeeper, and Calvin—addressed by all the Hugheses, including Reynolds, simply as Wilps—as house man and chauffeur.

When Reynolds entered the house, he noticed Mrs. Wilps descending the main staircase at a considerably slower pace than before. She wore a plain black dress as uniform. Reynolds greeted her casually, as if she were an older sister.

She replied, "Morning, Chewy," using the nickname she had given him and still used, the origin of which was his habit as a child of standing with her in front of the stove and chewing on the hems of her skirts while she was cooking. Being called Chewy didn't bother Reynolds, he rather liked it—only by Mrs. Wilps, of course. She said, "I finished ironing those shirts you wanted to take with you to Boston. They're on the lowboy by your bed."

Reynolds thanked Viora and asked the whereabouts of his mother and Wilps. He added that he needed time for a serious talk with his mother.

She scratched her head as she always did whenever a question was put to her, as if the question were a great puzzle and the answer a mystery. Reynolds knew it was not, Mrs. Wilps always knew where they were. At the same time, he noticed a few more streaks of gray in Mrs. Wilps' elaborately braided hair. He wondered how old she was. He was uncomfortable with the fact that he didn't know.

She said, "She's off fighting with the other members of the Art Museum board. Something about Germans, uh, German...somebodies. She told me this morning, but dang if I recall. They, the board members, are considering an exhibit of paintings by early 20th century Germans, and your mama hates them. As for a serious talk, I don't think so. She'll have a headache when she gets home. Always does after the Art Museum board."

When finally, Malvina stormed into the Manor House from the garage it was on a wave of muttered curses, as if she were caught in a rip tide, as if she were not the source of the tide but its captive. In her wake was Wilps, holding an umbrella over Malvina's head but silent, as he often was. Viora did their talking.

Malvina said, angry enough to stammer, "Those goddamned fools, those cowards, those…"

Viora, standing at the ready with aspirin and a glass of water, said, "Those German somebodies, ma'am?"

"Expressionists is what I said earlier, Viora," Malvina said. "Expressionists, not somebodies, but yes, I hate abstract expressionists, especially the German abstract expressionists, but when I said fools and cowards, I was referring to the so-called *men* of the Art Museum board. Oh, they give me such a headache." She held her head between two hands to prevent it from falling off onto the floor.

"Yes, ma'am," said Mrs. Wilps, offering the tablets and water. "Here's what'll fix ya."

"Thank you, Viora. I'll lie down with my feet up and…"

"M'mah?" Reynolds.

She turned to him and really meant to be angry. Earlier that morning, when he failed to appear for breakfast and she found his bed hadn't been slept in, Malvina promised herself that she would reproach him. But just to look at him, so handsome even though he looked as if he had slept in his clothes, her anger evaporated like a breath in the cold morning air. She stood with arms akimbo and tried to grouse at him, but Reynolds never had any trouble reading her.

Malvina said, "Well, the prodigal son returns, does he?"

"Really, M'mah? We're getting biblical, are we? Because for one night I slept elsewhere?"

She took him by the arm and led him into her sitting room, not wanting the servants to overhear. She said in a stage whisper, "It's not where you slept, it's with whom."

"Now, M'mah," Reynolds said in his most unctuous tone. "Didn't you say you had a headache?"

"I do, I..."

"Well don't you think you ought to swallow those?" He indicated the aspirin and water Viora Wilps had given her. "They'll work better inside you than in your hand." Reynolds watched her swallow the tablets and wash them down with the water, after which he relieved her of the empty glass.

He said, "Now let's settle ourselves over there on the settee. There. Now lean back against me. Eyes closed? Good. I'll massage away the headache the way I always do." Malvina eagerly complied with his commands and he began drawing little circles with his fingertips against her temples. She breathed an audible sigh. When he thought she was sufficiently relaxed, he whispered in her ear, "Now please tell me why you were so rude to my girlfriend the moment you heard her name was Schermer."

Malvina sat bolt upright and turned to him, but Reynolds knew better than to back down; he was confident in his power to control the situation.

She made a face at him and said, "You're just like your father. You think you can twist me around your little finger."

I don't just think I can, dear M'mah, I know I can. He kept that thought to himself; he patted his chest, coaxing her to return for more massaging, which she did. Once she was back under the spell of his fingers, he said, "Now it's time you let me know what's between you and the Schermers. Whatever it is, I need to know it." Almost inaudibly, "…for reasons I'll be making clear shortly." Then louder, "And you need to make peace with it, whatever it is, and soon."

Malvina felt herself trapped between her determined son to whom she could deny nothing, and between a lot of unhappy memories that she preferred to leave moldering in the past. Still she understood, reluctance aside, that she couldn't escape without telling him something. But what was there to tell?

Hers was a privileged childhood, but not a happy one. The only child of the Lumber King. She believed herself to be an ugly duckling who had never become a swan. If Reynolds insisted on knowing the truth about *her*, well, that was it. And the truth about his father? From her first sight of him, Malvina had loved Brockton Hughes passionately, but he turned out to be a disappointed, discontented man, and Malvina's marriage to him had been a torment. She wondered how that knowledge would serve Reynolds. Not well, she worried, considering how strained the relationship had always been between father and son.

Perhaps a little knowledge of family history would do him no harm. Or perhaps it would do more harm than good? She shrugged, wondered.

Malvina rested against her son's chest, and gazing upward, talked as if the words she was saying were written on the ceiling:

"I was seventeen when I first met your father. I had heard of him, of course, but I first laid eyes on him at seventeen. He was home from Princeton, a senior student I think he was at the time, and I was a junior at Choate. It was about this same time of year, Fall, and we were home on Thanksgiving holiday. The boys were roughhousing on the grounds behind Worthington Manor, scrambling and yelling, steam coming off their young bodies like blue-white clouds; they were engaged in a pickup game of soccer. We girls—my friends from Exeter and Andover and I— we were there for no other reason than to ogle the boys. Of course.

"I recall," she said with a sigh, "all those young stallions chasing after that soccer ball at full gallop across the green. But, oh, your father…he was tall and strong. Brock Hughes in those days was oh so tall and strong and handsome.

"Anyway, before I was to return to Wallingford, Connecticut, Mother asked me what I might want for Christmas. I told her I wanted Brock Hughes. In jest? Not really. I definitely wanted Brock Hughes. And much to my joy, Daddy—your GrandP'pah Strickland—set about to get me that very thing.

"By that Christmas my father and Brock's father, your two GrandP'pahs, had begun making arrangements for the merger of our families into a dynastic alliance the likes of which hadn't been seen since the time of the great Kings and Emperors of Europe. And by summer vacation of that year the alliance was all but a *fait accompli*. Your father and I were almost inseparable that summer, and it was…"

Although Reynolds hated to interrupt the unwinding of this heretofore untold tale, he couldn't help but interject, "Inseparable? If you mean what I think you mean—"

"No, I don't mean what you think I mean, you naughty little boy," Malvina replied. "This was a different time I'm speaking of. It wasn't like now. 'Nice' girls, if I can refer to myself and my peers in that way, nice girls preserved our greatest gifts for the marriage bed." Malvina moved as if to sit up. "If you're no longer interested in hearing this…"

Reynolds held her back. "By all means continue. Please."

"Returning to school was a letdown, let me tell you it was, after that glorious summer. I didn't want to go back, and I said so, but Brock insisted, and of course my parents did too. But Brock sent me spinning when he said to me… It was on one of the last nights of vacation, in late August when he said to me, 'The editor-publisher of the *New Countian Magazine* must have a wife who is well-educated.' A definite marriage proposal. Even if such a thing as the *New Countian Magazine* didn't yet exist, he meant it *would* exist one day. You didn't know that about your father, did you? Nobody did. He hadn't told anyone of this except me. His dream was to become an editor/ journalist. His idol was William Shawn. You know of whom I speak?"

Reynolds said, "William Shawn? Of course, M'mah. Who hasn't heard of the longtime editor of *New Yorker Magazine*?"

"He was your father's idol. His intention, your father's, was to move to New York City or Washington D.C. and learn the workings of the magazine business while I was getting my college degree. Then we would both return here to the County, get married, start a family and a new weekly, both at the same time. That was his dream. He had high hopes and big ideas in those days."

Reynolds said, "I gather GrandP'pah Hughes had other ideas."

"He did, and so did GrandP'pah Strickland."

"I don't see what all this has to do with the Schermers."

"Nothing and everything to do with the Schermers, dear boy, if you'll be patient.

"With those dreams of your father's and his talk of marriage to console me, I returned to Choate. When next I saw your father, that would have been at the 1961 Thanksgiving break. I think it was 1961. Oh, whenever. When next I saw him, he was a broken, beaten, dispirited young man. Between his father and mine, they had beaten the dreams out of him like you would beat dust from a rug. He had given up becoming a magazine owner-editor, and it seemed as if he had given me up, too. I learned from Mother, who learned it from… oh, what does it matter who she learned it from. Without going into a lot of details that don't really matter, it seems that between our glorious summer and that following Thanksgiving, your father had a number of brief, ahem, shall we call them, romances? With several not very respectable girls from the *other side* of town. And one of them was named—"

Finally, Reynolds got it. He said, "Schermer."

"Yes. Katherine Schermer, your girlfriend's… What's her name, Clovis? Her mother."

"Cloris, M'mah, Cloris Schermer."

"The very name makes me shudder, makes my head start to pound again. She tried to steal your father from me, and if it weren't for your GrandP'pahs, God rest both of their souls, she might have succeeded."

Reynolds said, "From what you've said, it seems to me P'pah was not without guilt in that regard."

This propelled Malvina into a sitting position. She said, "No, I didn't mean to imply that. I…"

"Now I wonder, M'mah. If the situation were somehow reversed, if P'pah had tried to steal a Schermer away from you, would you blame me for my father's sins? I'm sure you wouldn't blame me, but that's what you're doing to Cloris, blaming her for *her* mother's sins."

It took a moment for Malvina to untangle that verbal knot and, when she had, another moment to muster the courage to admit there was truth in what he said. When finally she did, peering into her son's soft brown eyes, she said, "If I see her again, I'll apologize."

"Not *if*, M'mah. *When*. I guarantee you'll see her again. We're talking about the woman I intend to marry. We're talking about your intended daughter-in-law."

Malvina grabbed onto her son's arm for support; she felt ill. She was on a rough sea and her ship was taking on water.

Chapter 14

Love Stain

Cloris couldn't decide what to wear. Early that morning, standing naked except for a bra and panties in front of the full-length mirror in her bedroom, she wondered, *What does one wear to an appointment with a divorce lawyer? Black widow's weeds, as if the marriage had died and you were going to its funeral? Or should she climb into an iron suit of armor like Joan of Arc, ready for a joust with horse and lance, ready to wage a pitched battle?* She decided that what was appropriate had to be located somewhere between those two extremes.

She chose a pant suit of royal blue—darker blue was closer to what she had in mind, but royal was what she owned, so royal blue would have to do. With a dash of color in a silk scarf at the neck to soften the effect, she decided. Regretfully she had no matching shoes, the black pumps with two-inch heels was the best her closet had to offer. The extra height might come in handy, she thought, and it wouldn't be hard walking afterward from the lawyer's office to keep her luncheon date with Meredith Goodlyn.

It was, after all, only a short walk from the lawyer's office on Main Street to *Chez Stanlí on* Otterman. No surprise, since everything is a short walk from everything else here. Rinky-dink of a Downtown.

Word got around at the previous week's meeting of the County Garden Club that no one who was anyone patronized *Offutt's Tearoom* any more. On hearing that, Cloris thought she might reserve a table at the *Tearoom* for the next get together with her old friend and college roommate. Not that either one of them would have chosen tea over an alcoholic beverage, nor were they particularly fond of tiny egg salad sandwiches on white bread with the crusts cut off, a staple served by Olive and Petunia, the spinster Offutt Sisters. But the thought of there being few if any eavesdroppers loomed large for Cloris in her present state. Still, the idea of Meredith making a grand entrance into the *Tearoom* dressed in one of her inevitably outrageous outfits gave Cloris second thoughts. The shock would be too much, Petunia would have to call an ambulance for Olive. Or vice versa. Besides, *Offutt's Tearoom* was directly across Maple Avenue from Reynolds' dental office, and Cloris didn't think she could handle running into her husband or anyone else from there.

So, Cloris had called *Chez Stanlí*, though she knew the last thing she needed was a reservation in mid-afternoon; she was assured by Monsieur Stanlí himself, in his phoniest French accent, that the table for two in the far corner of the dining room favored previously by the *cher Madame* Hughes and her *tres cher amie* would be reserved for one p.m. She is seated now at that little corner table facing the door.

Cloris hadn't expected *Chez Stanlí* to have changed since her last visit, and it hadn't—it was as tastelessly glitzy as ever, a Francophile's nightmare. The silence was more than a little bit disconcerting. Cloris recognized it as the silence of an establishment in its death throes.

The proprietor himself, Monsieur Stanlí—a.k.a. Stanley Greenbaum—greeted her at the door and ushered her to the corner table she had requested. He hadn't changed either, at least not for the better. The comic effects of goatee and waxed moustache were still present, but despite them Stanlí looked more care-worn, as if the killing silence had aged him. Cloris noticed for the first time a gap in his smile where a bicuspid or molar was missing.

She was about to take her first sip from a flute of *Prosecco* that she had ordered, hoping its effervescence would lift her spirits, when Meredith came through the front door. She was wearing a pink, hip-length canvass rain jacket with a hood. Cloris could sense the few people in the place holding their breath, anticipating the removal of that outer garment. When she did remove it—shock and awe.

Meredith was clad—partially clad, some might say—from neck to ankles in silver gray. The tightest pants anyone had ever seen, pants so tight…well, and a top with no back and a v-shaped front. 'V' for victory? Or freedom?

Cloris didn't know about victory, but Meredith's breasts had lots of freedom. She looked as if she had been torn from the cover of an issue of *Playboy* magazine.

Cloris stood and they air-kissed. She said to her friend, "How did you manage to stuff yourself into those pants?"

"And how are *you*, sweetie?" Meredith replied. "Don't think it was easy, it wasn't. But the fabric is flexible."

And fairly transparent, Cloris couldn't help noticing.

Monsieur Stanlí approached, his eyebrows dancing in a suggestive way he had seen some Frenchman do in an old movie.

He said, "A pleasure to see you once again, *Mademoiselle*."

A pleasure to see every inch of you, Cloris thought.

Meredith ordered a glass of sauvignon blanc and launched into a word-for-word report of her latest encounter on the internet.

She said, "…and so he's like, 'Okay, we'll meet at *Froggie's Bar* on Fourth Street,' and I say, 'My ass we'll meet at *Froggie's*, we'll meet at the *Juice 'n Java* on Main.'"

"You didn't say…"

"The hell I didn't. I said, 'I've had the bar scene up to here. I do the internet thing to avoid hanging out in bars, and you want me to meet you in a bar? My ass I will.' And he…" Meredith stopped. "Why the long face, Clo?"

Cloris shook her head to put Meredith off, but Meredith knew her old roomie well, guessed what Cloris's sad face meant. She thought, *uh oh*.

Cloris could not face her friend's eyes. She made circles with her finger around the rim of her wine flute, making the glass sing. When she finally had the courage to look up, she mustered enough courage to take a breath and come out with, "I think Reynolds is having an affair, no, I know he is. I've been to see a lawyer. I just came from there."

"Reynolds? You mean your husband the dentist?" To Meredith, the idea that anyone would have an affair—a romance, for God sakes—with a dentist was ludicrous. Of course, she didn't want to sound that way to Cloris. She said, "How do you know, how did you find out?"

Cloris said, "She's, whoever she is, is sending me little hints on his shirt collars. With her…"

One of Stanlí's waiters intruded. His southwestern Pennsylvania accent was fierce.

He said, "Would y'uns like to see a menu nile?"

There was a gap in his grin too, just like his boss's. Cloris wondered, Could a restaurant's failing cause decay? Was there a madman with a pair of pliers loose on the premises? Cloris also wondered if, as a dentist's wife, she had fallen into her husband's habit of staring at everyone's mouth. Her chest ached, right beneath the breast bone. She *was* a dentist's wife. He was a Hughes, certainly he was, but he *was* a dentist and she *was* his wife.

Meredith gave an exasperated sigh, Cloris was again making circles on the rim of her glass.

Meredith said to the young waiter, "Keep the menus. Bring a large Southwest Salad and two plates. We'll split it. And that gasoline your boss calls vinai-grette? On the side." She pressed her bosom and said, "Now put your eyes back in your head and get lost."

She returned her attention to Cloris and said, "You were saying how you know."

"Oh, there's no doubt. She's leaving little dabs of her perfume on his shirt collars. To let me know she's taking possession. I recognized it right away." The look she aimed at Meredith was more than a little bit accusatory. "The kind you always wear."

Love Stain. A startled Meredith made an involuntary move toward her ears, where she always daubed a bit of her scent—left wrist, right wrist, left lobe, right lobe, cleavage. Why was the idea of an affair with a dentist so outrageous? She didn't know, but for her it was.

She said, "Honey, you don't think it's me messing around with your Reynolds, do you? I wouldn't, Clo, you know I wouldn't. Clo!"

Cloris, all confusion, shaking her head yes, shaking her head no, nodding, shrugging. She said, "Yeah, no, I don't know. What do I know?" Then she seemed to get a grip on herself, reached across the table and grasped Meredith's hand. "No, when I can think rationally, I know you wouldn't. You told me once how afraid you were of dentists, that you'd open your mouth for a dentist if you had to, but not your legs. You'd never ever open your legs for a dentist. When I'm rational, I remember that," she said, sounding contrite.

"Honey," Meredith said, "it's not even expensive stuff. *Love Stain* can be had on sale, half off, at *Macy's* and *Penney's*."

So, this mystery woman is after Cloris's man and for some reason that mystery woman wants Cloris to know she's moving in on her.

"These little hints you've found, you think she's leaving them intentionally? You're sure?"

"A spot here, a spot there, sometimes no spot at all, that would be accidental. But at the same spot every time, near the left point of his shirt collars? Oh, yeah, it's intentional. It's like the bitch is challenging me to a duel."

"A duel, hmm," Meredith said, her gaze aimed off into the middle distance in search of an answer. What she found out in the distance was determination. "More than just a challenge to a duel, Clo," she said. "I think she considers it a game. Yes, she's challenging us to a game, and I think it's our turn to make a move. How do we respond?"

Her use of 'we' startled Cloris. She said, "How did this become 'we' all of a sudden?"

"Not all of a sudden, sweetie. From the day we met in Happy Valley, I've been on your side. I'm on your team. So, tell me, what's our first move?"

Cloris thought she had already made the first move and she said so. Meredith wasn't sure she had.

She said, "Have you decided whether or not you still love the guy? Do you want to hold onto him or dump him? If you can get a decent settlement, as I did, would you rather be rid of the cheating bastard?"

Cloris said, "In the latter case..."

"In the latter case, then and only then do you get a lawyer."

"But I already have. I told you, I was there this morning." She found his card in her jacket pocket. She read from it, "Seamus Gallagher, Attorney-At-Law, 1400 Main Street, second floor..." She tossed the card on the table; it landed on a wet spot. She saw that Meredith was shaking her head. "What?"

Meredith said, "When you're *really* sick, what do

you do? You get yourself a Jewish doctor. When you're really pissed off at your husband, you get a Jewish lawyer, not an Irishman. Definitely not an Irishman."

Confusion. Knowing her friend through and through, Cloris realized she was supposed to laugh at the blatant racial slur, but what she felt like doing, she felt like crying. She shook her head, shrugged then with a sigh she gave up to the flood of tears that had built up in her. They made tracks down her cheeks.

"Aw, honey." Meredith handed her napkin across to her weeping best friend.

She said, "Well, it's evident we still love him and want to keep him..."

Cloris nodded yes, we do.

"So. First thing tomorrow morning I'll send out feelers among my friends at work. There are some wild women in chemical engineering. You'd be surprised. I've got friends who know the bar scene in this County, you'd swear they were undercover narcs. If your husband has been seen... Anyway, for now we'll forget about getting a Jewish... Speaking of the devil."

Monsieur Stanlí himself appeared, balancing a Southwest salad in one hand and two place settings in the other. When he was able to drag his eyes away from Meredith's mostly exposed breasts, he began clearing a landing place for the huge bowl of salad in the center of the tiny table.

He was about to say *Bon Appétit,* but Meredith cut him off.

She said, "Listen, Stan. I underestimated the extent of our hunger. While we're working on the salad, bring us refills of our drinks and a couple of your infamous hamburgers. We've been challenged, and we need protein."

"Cloris added, "We need meat."

"You are referring to *zee fromage burgers*?"

Meredith said, "That's not *Velvetta* you put on them, is it?"

Stanlí was scandalized.

"Then, yes, the *fromage burgers*. And we'll have them rare, Stan. We're out for blood. Lots of blood."

CHAPTER 15

No One's About

It was being a stubborn, dry Spring. Those dark, heavy clouds that might have borne saving rains to Worthington County had abandoned it, only to dump their blessings on other counties in the more northerly parts of the State. Things had died as a consequence, among them a four-foot-high azalea in Judge Amos Gongaware's front yard. His favorite azalea. It was late in the planting season and still very dry, but the customer is always right. A replacement for the Judge's favorite azalea was at present a passenger in the truck bed of Bruno Maestromateo's green Ford F150.

The way through the Larchmont Plan to the Judge's residence led past the Hughes house, and Mattie pulled to the curb in front of it. There seemed to be no one about, at least no one was in sight. Which to Mattie was a concern, for the gardener hadn't seen anyone about for at least a week. *Where was the Missus*?

It was her habit, Mattie knew, to be outside snipping, watering, hoeing, aerating; tending her plants as if they were little children. Up with the sun and out early, that was her way, but not so for at least a week.

Mattie checked the row of mountain laurels that adorned the front of the house—dry, abandoned. Then he crossed the front lawn and took the path alongside the house. Stopped at the back gate. Silently. Standing at the gap in the left edge of the garden, in front of the hole that was left when they removed the dead yew, with her back to Mattie, unmoving, unaware of his presence—the Missus.

Mattie might have called out to her if he weren't a man who was quick to assess a situation, quick to discern a mood. His immediate instinct told him not to startle her, not to disturb her in any way, whatever possessed her. Then he saw her shoulders quiver and knew she was crying.

Yes, we've lost a the yew and she is taking it so hard, as if she's a lost something so precious. Leave her be, Bruno, he told himself. *Leave her be.*

He returned to his truck and pulled away.

Chapter 16

Packing Heat

*O**ver the river and through the woods**, but not to grandmother's house, not in a sleigh and not at Christmastime. It was August; the corn stalks were indeed high, but most of the ears had been picked and could be bought at a roadside stand for three bucks a bushel. Cloris was driving her new Toyota Corolla, and her good friend and old college roommate, Meredith Goodlyn, was her passenger.

They were winding their way northward along a two-lane State road through farms and forested land on their way to a town named after a former First Lady, EleaNOR RooseVELT. Norvelt, more a village than a town: a few collapsing barns and corn cribs, an empty silo, a cluster of tiny ranch-style dwellings, a derelict tractor abandoned in a front yard. But located on one side of the road in Norvelt was the headquarters of *Thompson Brothers Heating and Air Conditioning*. On the other side, the same Thompson Brothers were proprietors of the County's biggest and busiest gun store.

Cloris said, "You're sure what this friend of yours said is reliable? We've got the right woman?"

Meredith replied, "I said, a co-worker not a friend, but reliable? Definitely. This woman knows what's going on between the sheets in every bedroom in town. Believe me, we've got our mystery woman, we've got her dead to rights, and we're gonna deal with her once and for all."

She had suggested they dress Western-style, and although Cloris hadn't a clue as to why that fit into Meredith's scheme, she complied by wearing blue jeans, a long-sleeved cowboy shirt and the dusty Chukka boots she usually wore for gardening. Meredith had squeezed into a pair of very tight, black leather pants that left no room for underwear and left nothing to the imagination. She topped that with a frilly pink Mexican blouse with several buttons unbuttoned and a white *Stetson* hat that she had found in a costume shop.

Cloris said to her, "I don't remember Dale Evans looking anything like you do. And I still don't understand why we had to dress Western. We're going to a gun shop, not *The Grand Ole Opry*. I feel like an idiot, and you look like one."

"Never you mind, pardner," Meredith twanged. "You just play along with little ole Meredith and she'll get us a six shooter right quick."

Cloris rolled her eyes. She had no idea why a gun was needed and no idea how her eccentric friend intended to get one. But... she pulled in among the other cars lined up in front of Thompson's gun shop.

Right away things turned strange. Entering the shop at the same time as the women, a middle-aged man, as short as Cloris but twice as wide, raced to get to the door ahead of the women. Meredith thought maybe they were giving something away in the shop and only one was left and Fatso wanted it. Turned out he was only in a hurry to politely hold the door for them. Such a simple old-fashioned gesture seemed to disarm Meredith.

To say nothing of the effect of the place on both of them. There was no Western motif, actually no motif at all, just a long rectangle with a floor of hard wood planks and a ceiling of hammered tin. It looked as if it might have been a tavern in a previous iteration, but with a combination counter and showcase instead of a bar running the entire length of the room. On display in the showcase were boxes of every caliber of ammunition, small caliber weapons and lethal-looking knives. All four walls were peg-boarded; hanging from the peg boards were examples of every style and manufacture of firearm, short-barreled and long.

The place smelled of gun oil, cordite and male aggression; Cloris found it dizzying.

The Thompson brothers were behind the counter tending bar, so to speak: taking weapons down from the wall, breaking them down, re-assembling them, pointing out features of sighting and loading; ramming home cartridge magazines, disengaging them; talking calibers, talking ranges, talking to customers who nodded as if wisely; magazines clacking, triggers clicking, customers ooh-ing, nervously giggling.

The brothers were huge men, twins, with hard-looking bellies draped over silver belt buckles. They had managed to pull black ICLite tee shirts over those huge bellies, and managed to get brown leather vests over the tee shirts, but the bellies defied them to button the vests. Peaked H&K ball caps topped off their sartorial splendor. They both had lots of facial hair and thin comb-overs under their caps.

Brother Tom looked down at Cloris and asked, talking around a wad he held between his lower lip and gums, asked what he could do for the little lady. Cloris, disinclining to speak, jerked a thumb in Meredith's direction, which was unnecessary, since Tom's attention had already shifted to admiring the frills on the front of Meredith's blouse.

He said to Meredith, "Any little thing I can show you, Sweetie?"

She replied, "Yeah, big boy, show me whatcha got…" Which grabbed brother Tim's attention. Meredith added, "…that'll fit in this." She dropped onto the counter what she had carried in from the car, a beaded clutch bag.

The two brothers stared at the dainty bag; they figured it to be less than half the size of a *Primanti's* sandwich. Brother Tim scratched his head. He said,

"We got a two-shot Derringer will fit. Fires .22 caliber rounds."

Brother Tom said, "Not much stopping power there, but it'll fit."

Meredith said, "You boys got us wrong. We're looking for something that'll just *barely* fit in the bag, with no room to spare for anything else except maybe for something the size of, say, a checkbook? Something big but with a short barrel. Something real ugly."

Cloris found her voice. She said, "Something that looks like it could blow a fair-sized hole in somebody."

The brothers looked at each other; Tom protruded his lower lip. He said, "A revolver, then." He turned to the wall behind him and removed a snub-nosed .38 caliber Policeman's Special. He said to Meredith, "Here, give 'er a feel."

"I don't need to give 'er a feel, try it for fit."

Cloris said, "God, but it sure is ugly."

Several customers gathered to watch the proceedings, and they seemed pleased when the ugly revolver managed to just fit inside the clutch bag. "Sold," said Meredith, to applause.

Brother Tim, who prided himself on his ability as a salesman, said, "That there piece comes with a box of .38 caliber ammo, gratis, free, our treat. But if it were me, I'd spring for a little extra and buy hollow points."

Brother Tom added, "Beefs up the stopping power a mite."

Meredith said, "Not necessary, thanks. We aren't interested in ammunition of any kind."

The brothers in chorus with a couple of puzzled on-lookers, "None?"

She replied, "No, none."

Once they had settled on the price of the weapon, with a discount for their not having taken the box of ammo, Cloris handed over her *Mastercard* and asked, "Aren't there any formalities? Background checks or anything?"

Brother Tom said, "Naw, maybe someday, but for now just fill out this here State form."

Brother Tim added, "Mind you, come next election remember to vote Republican."

It was now the following morning.

Act two of the drama that Meredith had devised was about to play out. Cloris drove slowly up the winding road that led to the top of McDonough Hill, the highest hill in the County, to the campus of Our Lady of Mercy College. The founding of this Catholic women's college had taken place almost simultaneously with the founding, some two hundred years before, of the County itself. One County wag was fond of saying that the College's ancient, ivy-covered red brick buildings, bell tower and especially its Gothic stone church seemed to him to be glowering down at the Courthouse, disapproving of the sins being perpetrated down below.

Of course, there were buildings of more contemporary design on the campus as well; one such modern edifice of sandstone and glass on the western edge of the campus happened to be Cloris's destination—the B. Reynolds Hughes Memorial Field House. The Field House had been donated by the Hughes Family Foundation and designed for the exclusive use of the Athletic Department. In one immense rectangle and its surrounding grounds, there were all the desired facilities: outdoor playing fields, two indoor gymnasiums and an Olympic-sized swimming pool; changing rooms, locker rooms, shower rooms, dressing rooms and office space for several coaches. The largest of the latter being that of Margaret Skatell, who doubled as basketball coach and Athletic Director.

After leaving her car in a vacant spot in the faculty parking lot, Cloris entered the Field House and headed for Coach Skatell's office. She was dressed in black skirt, white blouse and a loose, summer-weight red blazer with brass buttons. What she called ladies-that-lunch dressy. Instead of the usual purse over her shoulder, Cloris was carrying the beaded clutch bag. Her appointment was for eleven a.m. and she was right on time.

As she made her way along the corridors, Cloris noticed a lingering *something* in the air, not even strong enough to be called an odor but pervasive, like a barely audible hum. She wondered if there were a tangible thing you could call femaleness. It was a women's college, after all. Whatever it was, she found it oddly comforting.

Coach Skatell was already at her desk when Cloris arrived. She looked a little bit stressed. Not knowing the reason for their meeting but guessing, Cloris hoped.

There was a large window behind the coach's desk, so that she *could* have been watching a team of girls practicing field hockey; or she *could* have been admiring the collection of trophies of her past triumphs on the basketball court, which were on display in a showcase to the right of her desk; or she *could* have been studying the postings on the board to her left: game sites, play dates and practice schedules. But, no, she was doing none of those things. Instead she was seated at her desk with a smile fixed to her admirable—Cloris had to admit—very admirable if somewhat beefy face, and staring down at Cloris.

The late morning sun shone through the window behind the coach, setting her helmet of blond hair aglow. She was big even by women's basketball standards: she was tall and broad, with an admirable bosom that was apparent even though she was dressed in loose, gray workout clothes. Cloris had to admit that a man might find her hard to resist. Cloris had to look up to see her face directly, even though the coach was seated. What a pain in the neck.

Cloris broke the ice, "Coach Skatell, I..."

"Call me Peg, please, or Coach Peg. Everybody does." The fixed smile never left her face.

"Coach Skatell," Cloris said pointedly, "I appreciate your finding time for me, and I promise I won't keep you long."

She would keep that promise, Cloris told the coach, because she had a lunch date with her husband.

"You've met my husband? Dr. Reynolds Hughes?"

The coach squirmed uncomfortably in her chair.

Cloris said she wanted to let Coach Skatell know how pleased and excited she was that Our Lady of Mercy College's varsity team had won that year's Women's Diocesan Basketball Tournament. And how proud it made her to see film clips of their victory broadcast on Channel 3 TV's 11 o'clock sports news.

"That's precisely why I asked for this meeting."

Coach Skatell looked even more uncomfortable than before when Dr. Hughes' name was mentioned, but she visibly relaxed at the mention of the basketball tournament.

Cloris continued, "We thought, that is, my husband and I thought the girls' uniforms looked awfully shabby on TV, and we thought the Hughes Memorial

Foundation could well afford to donate the cost of new uniforms for next year's team."

Cloris was prepared, she said, as managing trustee of the Foundation, to write a check to the Athletic Department to cover the cost of new basketball uniforms.

"I have my checkbook right here," she said.

From where it had been resting in her lap, Cloris took the beaded clutch bag, unzipped it and placed the open bag on the desk in front of the coach.

"That's, uh, that's awfully gen…"

Whoops!

When Cloris slipped the checkbook from the bag, the revolver slipped most of the way out, too.

Coach Peg couldn't help seeing it and couldn't help interpreting its meaning. Her eyes went wide and she turned a paler shade of white. She was silent except for a choking sound.

Cloris finished writing the check, then replaced the checkbook in the bag and used a single finger to shove the pistol back in.

Handing over the check, Cloris said, "This'll cover it?" No reply. "I won't have to trouble myself with this matter any further? Good."

The coach had not yet found her voice; for Cloris's money, it could stay lost. She stood, wished the coach a nice day and returned to her car.

As she took the winding drive down McDonough Hill, she thought about her friend Meredith. She was definitely crazy, but like a fox.

CHAPTER 17

The Credit Union

*A*mazing! Cloris thought as she drove toward the downtown, *How cool imagination is.* All this time since she had watched her mother's coffin trundled along a conveyor belt into the crematory oven—horrified by the machinelike callousness of it—and still she imagined she smelled something burning in her car.

As usual, she would open *Tipson's Posies* in a few hours—Mrs. Tipson's arthritis made mornings impossible for the poor old lady—but first she had an appointment to attend the inventory of her mother's safe deposit box. Salvatore Gongaware, Trust officer at the local branch of the *Federal Credit Union*, volunteered to preside at the State-mandated formality. Not that Cloris expected to find anything valuable in Katherine Schermer's safe box, but she thought, go tell that to the Department of Revenue.

Cloris hung a left at the intersection of Main and Otterman Streets, passed the vast parking lot of

Minutemen's National, and finally squeezed her car between two pickup trucks in the tiny lot provided by the Credit Union. Leave it to her mother to patronize the least convenient financial institution, but the only one in the County in which the Hughes family did not have an interest. Just for spite.

At 8:30 a.m. the Trust Officer, Sal Gongaware, was waiting at the glass front door to hold it for Cloris. He was a born-and-bred Worthington Countian, like Cloris, and a classmate of hers in high school. The wise guys in the class had hung the sobriquet 'Icky' on him, because he was an Ichabod Crane look alike—a bent flagpole of a body, a protruding Adam's apple and a timid spirit. Cloris knew Icky had been sweet on her and suspected he still was. No wedding band on the finger of his left hand. She felt bad about having turned down the opportunity to be his date for the senior prom. He was a sweet guy but icky back then; a sweet guy but icky now. It really was nice of him to do this so early for her; in gratitude, Cloris decided to use his real name.

She said, "Nice to see you, Sal. I appreciate the early hour."

He replied, "Any time for you, Cloris. You know that."

Used as Cloris was to seeing her ex-husband dressed in custom-tailored suits valued at thousands of dollars, she had to admit that the navy-blue number Sal was wearing fit his station in life, if not his awkward frame. Icky was icky, not a Hughes man. Cloris actually found the contrast refreshing.

He escorted her to the safe deposit vault, explaining the procedure as they went. So proud of his knowledge, it lengthened his stride. Cloris had to hustle to keep up with him. The bank was required by State law, he said, to place a seal over a safe deposit box as soon as they were made aware of a box holder's demise—he had made an exception and postponed it until now, for Cloris—and they were required to have a representative present when the contents of the box was inventoried. Said bank representative—in this case, him, Icky said—was then required to file a Form REV-485 with the Department of Revenue, on which form the representative certified as to the value of the box's contents.

He said, "The Tax Man will have his due, Cloris. There's no denying him. If your mom has the family jewels hid in there...."

Knowing how Katherine Schermer used to denigrate her husband—Cloris's father, Jack Schermer—calling him a worthless bum who never amounted to anything, Cloris wouldn't have been surprised to find 'the family jewels' in that box.

Cloris said, "I don't expect to find anything in the box except some old papers: the deed to mother's house, the paid-up mortgage, the closing papers when we sold the house before moving mother into the Rehab facility, stuff like that. No money and nothing valuable. Mother hardly had a pot to… you know. She would've been eligible for food stamps if she weren't too proud to apply for them. And she wouldn't take a cent from me, to her that was Hughes money."

Sal said, "She was one tough old bird, eh? Well, God rest her."

He removed the adhesive seal over the lock and used two keys to unlock the box; he slid it out and placed it on the table in front of them. Lifted the lid.

They discovered that Cloris was right, nothing in the box was valuable; they found only a stack of documents, some yellowed with age: the deed to the house, the closing papers, mother's birth certificate, Cloris's, an insurance policy cancelled due to unpaid premiums. Not even mortgage papers.

"You were right, Cloris," Sal said. "Nothing valuable. I can testify to that effect on the form to the Revenue Department. You wanna lease this box and keep these papers here, or take them with you?"

She might as well take them, she told him; she could store the papers in the safe box she owned at *Minutemen's Bank*. He frowned at that.

As he was replacing the empty box in its slot, Cloris glanced at her birth certificate, which she assumed was a copy, since she had the original—her mother had told her she had the original—at home. But Cloris noticed a discrepancy between that one and the one she now held in her hand: the line requiring the name of the father was blank. She called this to the banker's attention.

He said, "No sweat, Cloris. That line is often blank, I see that a lot. It only means the mother assumed financial responsibility for the hospital stay and didn't immediately give the hospital the father's name. No biggie, they fill that information in later."

Cloris said, "Guess that's why the one I have at home is different, has my dad's name, Jack Schermer, on that line."

Sal said, "You say, Jack Schermer? I never met your dad."

"Neither did I. He was killed in the war, before I was born."

"Which one? I mean, which war was he killed in?"

Cloris realized she didn't know, she hadn't had the courage or curiosity to confront her mother for answers, had never thought it made any difference. She shrugged.

Sal carefully took the yellowing deed to the Schermer house from Cloris's hands.

"You might consider donating this deed to the County Historical Society. We can use more stuff about those old houses on the Flats. This deed is sure as hell old enough."

Cloris stood close to Icky as they perused the old document. Was it her nearness that caused his Adam's Apple to bob? Or was it what he read on the deed? He scratched his head and harumphed. She asked him to clarify.

He said, "The original owner was B. Reynolds Hughes Sr.—that was your husband's grandfather, Cloris."

"I know that, Icky."

"But look. He transferred ownership of the house to Katherine Schermer—your mother..."

"I knew that, too."

"But for the sum of only one dollar. Huh. No wonder there's no mortgage in the box. There never was a mortgage. How strange."

It was indeed strange. Cloris decided to look into it further, do some research, if necessary, ask around. She could be a bulldog when her curiosity was peaked. On second thought, however, she wondered if anyone still alive would know anything. She doubted it. Oh, well.

She retrieved the deed from the banker's hands, and thanked him profusely. In doing so her hand inadvertently touched his sleeve; she watched him blush. She thanked him again and left the vault.

So, it seemed that before she was born, the house on Harrison Avenue had been gifted to her mother by the Hughes family. Gifted. She wondered why. What had gone on back then? Cloris was beginning to think a lot more had gone on than she had ever dreamed.

CHAPTER 18

A Fiction

C loris knew she could save a few steps if she entered the Courthouse Annex by the door that fronted onto Main Street, just cater-cornered from *Posies*, and immediately exited by the back door onto Pennsylvania Avenue. But it was such a glorious day, such a cloudless sky, such a warming sun on her face, a wonderful day for a walk on her lunch hour. And she had the usual options: if she happened to be in a dark mood, a *left* turn out of *Posies*, going a block south on Main and a right down Second Street would take her along the south side of the Courthouse, the dour gothic old Courthouse.

But instead today's bright mood called for a *right* turn out of *Posies*, going two blocks north on Main, then a stroll through the tiny parklet in front of the Annex and a walk along the Annex's modern, yellow brick north side to reach Pennsylvania Avenue. Her destination was the U.S. Army Recruiting Center.

It was not her intention to enlist.

For the first time in her life she was free to satisfy her curiosity about her father and his military service without her mother impeding her, but without her mother as a source of information, she had no idea where to go. She was aware of the Recruiting Center's location since it was across Pennsylvania Avenue from the Public Library and next door to the *Christian Science Reading Room*. She had seen men and women in uniform coming and going from there—from the Recruiting Center, not the *Reading Room*. She hoped they could answer her questions; if not, perhaps they could tell her where answers could be found.

The Downtown streets at noon, especially on the north-south Main Street, were noisy and often smelly with traffic, but Cloris enjoyed walking them despite the roar of cars, pickup trucks and 18-wheelers. She enjoyed it because of the people she would meet and those who would greet her—so many friends.

No sooner had she thought that than Biffy Teaberry came out for a breath of air from his *Men's Big & Tall*. Biffy waved to Cloris and called a greeting to Woogie Pratt, standing on the sidewalk outside of *Beltz's Hardware*. Such nicknames we tacked onto each other in school, she thought: Biffy, Woogie, Icky. It gave her a chuckle. Did the girls have nicknames? She imagined some of the wise-assed boys had a nickname for her. Cloris wasn't the first girl in the class to wear a bra, but she was the first one to really need to wear one.

She called hi to Biffy, waved to Woogie, peered into the storefront window of the *Reading Room*—deserted, as usual—and finally arrived at the Army Recruiting Center.

She was greeted by the approach of a 40-some-thing soldier, not much taller than Cloris but, as she expected, very neatly dressed in a dark green, worsted wool uniform. He marched toward her and offered his hand to be shaken. There was a colorful array of medals on his proud chest and lots of stripes on the sleeves of his uniform coat. His name tag read, **Moats**. An unfamiliar name for these parts, Cloris thought, not from around here. Cloris shook his calloused hand, resisting an urge to salute him.

The soldier said, "Sergeant-Major Michael Moats at your service, Ma'am. Welcome to the Recruiting Center," in a voice that convinced Cloris that she was indeed in good hands. He added, "It'd be my pleasure to discuss your future with the United States Army." Cloris was convinced he was sincere about that, too.

He had a pleasant clean-shaven face, a ruddy complexion, brilliantly-white capped front teeth, a drinker's nose and a salesman's easy manner. Cloris was wary of such types, but it was obvious to her that the Army's Human Resources Department had employed the right man.

He ushered Cloris to a seat in a small room that was more lounge than office. She was offered the beverage of her choice, which she refused with thanks.

She wondered if she was in the right place, her bet would have been, no. But what the hell, why not give it a try?

She said, "Well, Sergeant... you said, Moats? Well, Sergeant Moats...how to put this? Well. I was told by my mother before she passed away..." The Sergeant-Major was sorry to hear that. "...before she passed away that my father had died in the war. I was wondering how I could find out more about his time in the military."

The Sergeant said, "Do you kind of get the feeling you're in the wrong place, Ma'am? Sherlock Holmes isn't stationed here."

Had that feeling from the moment I walked in, Cloris thought. She said, "Yes, I see that."

Moats said, "So. You know you're in the wrong place, but your daddy was an Army guy so you figured..." He stopped when Cloris shook her head. "You're not even sure your dad was in the Army? He was maybe in the Navy or the Air Force? Haven't you found any paperwork? In the military, there's always paperwork, believe me. Discharge papers or...No, you said he was killed, so there would be a death certificate."

Cloris said, "No paperwork, no nothing, not even a birth certificate."

Sergeant-Major Moats started to wonder if her father was maybe a figment of her imagination, but he kept that disturbing thought to himself. He knew there existed in St. Louis, Missouri, a Government facility that maintained a file on every person who ever served in the United States military. A madhouse jammed with paper. But he was pretty sure that a qualified relative—spouse, child, brother or sister—was entitled to access the file of their soldier. He told this to Cloris.

He said, "It's a huge storehouse of public records."

Cloris replied, "St. Louis is a long way off."

"True. There's prob'ly a special form that you have to fill out with the pertinent information about you and your soldier, then you mail it to St. Louis." The Sergeant expected there would be an interminable bureaucratic delay, after which you would receive the information by return mail.

To that Cloris replied, "I don't have much information, in fact, hardly any at all. Only that he died in the war and that mother didn't like him very much."

"The Army won't want to know that she didn't like him very much, they won't give a damn about that, but it'll help to know which war he died in."

"I'm not sure which war he died in, I always assumed it was the Korean War, but I realize that's just an assumption on my part. I'm not sure." Cloris's admission surprised Moats; his brow went up. She added, "There have been so many wars, police actions, skirmishes, revolts, revolutions. An endless number, and mother would fly into such a rage whenever I tried to pin her down. I found it safer not to ask."

This was obviously a family thing of which the Sergeant-Major wanted no part. He suggested that Cloris start her search at the Courthouse Annex, where she could arrange to obtain her father's birth records and one of those special forms to send to the facility in St. Louis. Cloris thanked him and stood to leave.

He said, "I don't suppose you want to talk about a career in the Army?" He saw her frown. "I thought not. Our loss."

Cloris crossed Pennsylvania Avenue toward the back door of the Courthouse Annex to begin what she feared would take more time than her lunch hour.

* * *

Dinner at Worthington Manor had always been served at six p.m., a tradition begun at the behest of GrandP'pah Hughes and maintained by Mrs. Wilps under orders from Brockton Hughes, Reynolds' P'pah. The dinner hour changed only after B. Reynolds Hughes III, DMD MS in Periodontology, had separated from his wife and re-established residence in his mother's house. Most recently Mrs. Wilps would begin to serve only after Dr. Hughes—Chewy to her, that hadn't changed—had arrived home from his office Downtown, showered, dressed neatly of course but casually, and seated himself at table across from his M'mah.

Just as Mrs. Wilps was about to serve the soup course, Wilps himself entered the dining room. He too had changed his clothes, from chauffeur's hat and gloves to houseman's uniform of navy-blue blazer and gray slacks.

Wilps spoke directly to Malvina, his long-time employer, "Pardon the interruption, Ma'am, but there's an urgent call for the doctor. A young woman begs pardon but requires an immediate consult about her gums."

This brought a chuckle from Reynolds as he rose from his place at table, plucking the napkins from his lap.

Reynolds said, "It's not really an emergency, M'mah. It's Cloris."

There being no phone in the dining room, Reynolds excused himself and went to take the call in the kitchen. When he returned to the dining room, he was still chuckling.

Not thinking anything concerning that woman—she had never given up thinking of her as Cloris Schermer, despite the marriage to her son, and was thrilled now, thanks to the divorce, to continue calling her Cloris Schermer—nothing concerning that woman could possibly be funny, Malvina asked him what the call was about.

He replied, "She's spitting mad, Cloris is, over the bureaucratic ineptitude, the indolent behavior displayed by our County employees. Seems they are having difficulty locating any record of her father. No birth record, no death certificate, no record of his marriage to Katherine Schermer, nothing."

"But why is that...why is she calling you? You're not seeing her again, are you?"

Reynolds let his M'mah's question go unanswered. Instead he quoted Cloris to her and to Mrs. Wilps, who stood in the doorway between the kitchen and dining room:

"She said, 'To those bureaucratic sons of bitches in the County Courthouse, Jack Schermer never even existed.'"

The idea had never occurred to Malvina, any more than it had to anyone else, but when she paused a moment to consider it, she wished she had thought of it before. She felt it as a cold draft that chilled her to the bone. She got up from the table, threw down her napkin and shooed Mrs. Wilps into the kitchen—as if that would prevent her hearing, which it didn't.

She said to Reynolds, "I wouldn't be so quick to condemn the County clerks if I were you, dear. If they can't locate any record of Jack Schermer, well then...

"I never gave it a thought, and why would I have? Jack Schermer wasn't a part of my world; nor was Katherine, for that matter. All I ever knew about her was, she was a schemer. I wouldn't put it past Katherine Schermer's kind of person, schemer that she was. If having a husband was required to bolster her pride and maintain her respectability, why, she'd just up and invent one. Lord knows how low such a person would go if she were...if she were really in trouble. But to invent a husband? Sure. Reynolds, it wouldn't surprise me to learn that your ex-wife's father never actually existed. Can you believe it? Jack Schermer may have been a fiction. Well, now that I think of it, it wouldn't surprise me a bit."

CHAPTER 19

The Mausoleum

Wilps maneuvered the black Cadillac limousine between massive wrought-iron gates and slowly wound his way up the narrow drive to the top of the hill that overlooked the manicured grounds of Worthington County Cemetery. He eased to the curb nearest the massive Hughes Mausoleum. A granite edifice in the Neoclassic style that Malvina's deceased husband's father, B. Reynolds Hughes Senior, had built.

And inhabited, Malvina thought, *along with Grandmother Hughes. And my Brock now inhabits, too.*

Wilps helped her out of the limo. She stood beside the still-open car door, allowing herself time to adjust to the constant unsettling wind that swept across the hill. Malvina would have preferred not to know why GrandP'pah Hughes had chosen this spot for his resting place but, of course, she *did* know: he would have considered it his privilege to look down upon everyone else buried below him. *Besides, GrandP'pah Hughes never had to wear widow's weeds*, she thought, struggling to settle her skirts.

There was a grassy stretch of less than twenty yards between the road and the mausoleum; only a faint path had been worn in it. Malvina made a mental note to have a paved walk installed.

"I'll make use of your arm, Calvin, if you don't mind," she said. "I feel a bit unsteady this morning."

Wilps was startled speechless that she used his first name, didn't think she knew it. But he rarely ever said much, and Malvina hadn't expected a reply. She took his arm and they covered the ground together. She stopped at the knee-high fence that surrounded the building; she thanked Wilps—again using his first name—and dismissed him back to the car.

She stood before the fence's little gate; didn't open it. She had vowed after accompanying her husband's coffin into the mausoleum to never walk into that creepy place again. She figured, when she was carried in, it would be soon enough.

At that moment Malvina was angrier at her husband than she had ever been. *Brock can very well hear my thoughts from where I am*, she thought at the gate.

Although according to the death certificate, signed by the Worthington County Medical Examiner, Brockton R. Hughes II had died of congestive heart failure, Malvina Hughes knew that her husband had died of disappointment.

Disappointment in your father's bullying you into a business career that bored you, and disappointment in your father and my father, too, for bullying you into a marriage not of your choosing. To me, a woman you didn't love. I wanted you from the very moment I lay eyes on you, and they got you for me. And I had to live with the consequences. Your silences, your ennui, your philandering, your avoiding my touch as if you were brittle, your glazed stares through me as if I were transparent, made of glass.

I bore it all, accepted your ways as punishment for my wanting. I gave you a son, and I love him and live only to protect him. Now I must know. What have you done, Brockton Hughes? What have you done? Must you reach out from the grave to damage your son? I had forgiven all your trespasses, Brockton Hughes, but I can't, I won't forgive that. I will hate you, I will hate you to my dying day.

There was, of course, no reply. Malvina turned away from the mausoleum and looked toward the car with eyes clouded with confusion. Wilps saw and came running as fast as two old knees permitted. Offered Malvina his arm.

"Thank you, Calvin," she said. "You're a good man."

They made their way together back to the limousine.

Chapter 20

French Toast

It had been a dreadful, restless night for Cloris. Unable to find comfort in her empty bed, she abandoned it and wandered around the house, barefoot and dressed only in a cotton nightshirt, hoping to rid herself of the feelings of loneliness and abandonment, but finding only oppressive silence. Entering the recreation room, she snapped on the TV—The Tonight Show. She left it on, but without sound; it threw agitated, ghostly blue shadows on the paneled walls. Next the radio, on then off, finding herself equally impatient with talk and music.

Thinking comfort might be found in a view of the outdoors, she drew back the drapes to see the garden through the glass sliders. What a surprise. The patio and flower beds were hiding under a blanket of snow that obviously had begun to fall after she closed up for the night. The relentless silence of the snowfall had a gravity that frightened her. She hadn't realized before how lonely she had been. She shivered like a frightened little girl and wanted to run to her mother. Since when was there ever comfort in her mother's arms? Besides, mother had passed. It was the only time Cloris could remember having missed her.

It was now mid-morning of what promised to be a typical western Pennsylvania day—dreary and overcast. The snowfall had ceased before the sun came up, and as the morning progressed the temperature rose, until it was now well above the freezing mark. Cloris returned to the spot in the recreation room she had occupied during the night, to once again gaze out at the garden.

Yearning for Spring, relishing the thought of working the soil, setting annuals into warm compost, getting her hands dirty. She had thrown a robe over her nightshirt and slid her feet into slippers. A steaming mug of coffee in her fist did its best to elevate her oppressive mood, but watching the beautiful blanket of snow decay into slush was dragging her down.

Startled when the phone broke the silence, Cloris spilled coffee down the front of herself. But grateful to have the silence broken, no matter who was calling. 'Caller ID' said, WORTHINGTON MANOR.

Cloris picked up without saying anything. She heard only air and the sound of air molecules dancing along the wires. She listened intently, heard him breathing.

Finally. "Hello, hello. Cloris? Hello, is anyone there?"

"It's not anyone, Reynolds, It's me. Why are you calling? I'm not your wife anymore."

Along with everything else this morning, it depressed Cloris to find herself so very glad to hear Reynolds' voice. She would have liked to punish him by giving him a hard time, but she wasn't confident in her ability to do so.

He said, "I had a new patient yesterday."

"You're calling to discuss your dental practice?"

"No, I... Please, Cloris. It's just that it was that crazy college friend of yours, Meredith Goodlyn."

"She's not crazy," Cloris said, conceding, "Maybe a little eccentric."

"Well, her gums were fine."

There went Cloris's resolve. She almost laughed out loud. She said, "I didn't ask her to intercede on my behalf, Reynolds, I didn't suggest that Meredith see you. So, don't bother thanking me for the referral. I didn't."

"No, no, I didn't think that. It's not why I'm calling."

"Then why *are* you calling?" She was willing to wait a while for him to decide, if only he would say what she wanted him to. But he was taking so long. "Frankly, Reynolds, I haven't a clue."

"Frankly? What if I said I was lonely?"

No reply.

"Aw, not the silent treatment, Cloris, please. Frankly, I miss you," he said with a sigh that sounded like relief. What followed that admission came more easily: "I was hoping we might get together, you know, over coffee or a drink, something like that. If you…well, if you would like to."

She said, "I doubt it's appropriate for a divorced couple to be seen out together, I mean, so soon after a divorce. People jump to the wrong conclusions, don't they? About your intentions, if you get what I mean?"

He said, "No, I don't. I don't get what you mean at all. If I happen to miss you, then that's what they are. My intentions. I still…I mean, I do, I still love you, and…well, that's what my intentions are. Besides, what business are my intentions to anybody else but me and…and you. If you get what *I* mean."

Finally. She said, "I still think it's inappropriate for a recently divorced couple to be seen out together."

She let him chew on that for a few beats. She thought she could actually hear him grinding his teeth. She added in as docile a voice as she could manage, "You could… come over here."

"Did you…did I hear… uh… Now?"

"Well…yes. Why not?"

Cloris finished her coffee then headed for the *en suite* bath off the bedroom. She stood before the mirror. Hadn't been sleeping well and looked that way—she stuck her tongue out at herself.

Cloris hurriedly brushed her teeth and showered, then dressed only in bra and panties, she stood before her closet puzzling over what was appropriate to wear for a reunion with her recently ex-ed husband. She felt it was essential to strike the right pose. She didn't want what she was wearing to send the wrong message, that she was eager. Her first choice, instinctual rather than thoughtful, was a purple Adidas warm up outfit—she immediately rejected it as too easily slipped out of in the heat of passion. Her second choice, tight designer slacks, shirt and a cardigan sweater with lots of buttons, went too far in the opposite direction. She decided her third choice—relaxed jeans and one of Reynolds' old white dress shirts—was the perfect compromise, but she had to hurry to climb into them because she heard the automatic garage door come to life.

When she heard him enter from the garage to the kitchen, she couldn't stop herself from dashing down the stairs, and when she saw him standing by the kitchen door, looking awkward and unsure of himself, caution flew away on the wind and she threw herself into his arms. Catching her knocked a considerable amount of wind out of him, she was small but far from delicate. But he held on.

He said, panting, "Huh—Do I take it you've forgiven me?"

She replied, "Don't think that, Reynolds. I haven't, and I'm not sure I can forgive or forget. Ever." Then embarrassed at her own passion she whispered in his ear, "But please take me upstairs. Now."

He did.

After sex came sleep, which neither of them had managed to get much of since their hasty separation. They hadn't slept well, hadn't eaten well—Reynolds had lost five pounds. Nothing else seemed to have gone well either: the flowers at *Tipson's Posies* had tended to wilt, and patients had suffered needlessly in his usually steady hands.

They lay spooned together fast asleep for hours; when they finally came to, most of the afternoon was gone.

She said, "Reynolds, you have to let me go…"

"Uh-uh, never again."

"But I have to pee."

He dug his nose into the hair at the nape of her neck and breathed deeply of her scent. He said, "You smell so nice."

"You're tickling me. Make me laugh and you're gonna get wet."

He did finally release her and she fled naked to the bathroom. Returned quickly and saw that Reynolds hadn't moved from where he lay in the bed. She took that as an invitation to rejoin him. She snuggled in.

After a bit Reynolds said, "Y'know, Clo, I think we were too hasty getting a divorce."

Neither of them spoke for a minute, then Cloris replied, "What in particular makes you think that?"

They both laughed.

Out of the blue Reynolds said, "I'm so hungry right now, I could eat a horse."

"Could you eat French toast instead? With lots of sweet butter and maple syrup. And lots of coffee?"

Of course, he could, they were his favorites. They hopped out of bed, retrieved terrycloth robes from the closet and headed down to the kitchen.

Now the French toast was gone, and the talk began over second mugs of coffee.

Reynolds said, "I've learned a lot about my parents and about me. I finally got M'mah to open up about my father."

"You *know* how I feel about your M'mah, Reynolds."

"I do, but in this case, she deserves a lot of credit. She told me so much I didn't know about him, and she suffered a good deal in the telling. But she saw me making the same mistakes P'pah made, and she wanted to set things right."

"If that's the case…"

"There was a lot of unhappiness in Worthington Manor, Cloris, unhappiness that I never noticed. M'mah was very unhappy; I never saw that. I *did* see that P'pah was an unhappy man, but I had no idea why. I thought he had everything a man could want—money, power, a loving family. But no. I found out GrandP'pah Hughes convinced P'pah to give up his dreams."

Cloris said indignantly, "He gave up my mother."

"You knew about that?"

Cloris nodded. "Mother told me before she died. She didn't tell me much, and what she *did* tell me I had to drag out of her, but she told me that she loved your father, and he gave her up to marry your mother. Threw her over. That's why she couldn't stand to hear the name, Hughes. Couldn't stand me dating you, couldn't stand me marrying you."

"He dated several women, not just your mother, Cloris. And he threw them *all* over to marry M'mah. According to her." He said, shaking his head, "I had no idea."

Reynolds helped her clear the dinette table and offered a hand with the dishes. He said, taking a towel from a drawer by the sink, "You wash and I'll dry, like we used to, okay?" Cloris gave him a look. He said, "Like we used to, Clo? Please. I never gave a thought that I might be hurting you. I never meant to, and I never will again, I swear. Please, Clo. I want everything to be the way it used to be. I need it to be. Okay? You wash and I'll dry?"

She loved Reynolds so much, loved him too much to refuse him entirely, Cloris knew that, and his contrition did seem sincere. She would have to find a way to forgive him. But forget? Never. And she decided to keep him squirming on the barbs of the hook a long time before she let him off.

She made a show of looking at the wall clock. She said, "Undoubtedly Mrs. Wilps and your *M'mah* are expecting you for dinner at Worthington Manor."

"Please don't mock me, Cloris."

He hinted that several pairs of his pajamas remained neatly folded in the armoire upstairs in the bedroom.

She thanked him for the reminder. She said, "I meant to donate the things you left behind to the Little Sisters of the Poor. I'll see to that tomorrow." But then she laughed, giving him hope.

In a few minutes she aimed him toward his BMW and gave him a push. As the garage door closed behind him, she smiled and waved—giving him hope that he'd be invited back.

Chapter 21

Family

Calvin Wilps, houseman and chauffeur, was fond of joking that if an ant were to fart anywhere in Worthington Manor, his wife Viora's hearing was so keen she would hear it loud as if a bomb had gone off. Maybe so.

From a place in the kitchen between the stove and the chopping block, Viora Wilps heard the tread of someone tiptoeing down the main staircase. It was a tread she recognized, she had heard the same person's tread many a time sneaking down from his bedroom in pretend hide-and-seek games—of course it was Chewy. A grin lit up her rather time-worn face—as she had caught the child, she would catch the man.

By the time he had reached the foot of the stairs, Mrs. Wilps was there to intercept him. He was dressed casually enough—for him—in light canvas shoes, designer jeans, a green polo shirt and a camel-colored jacket, but he was carrying an overnight bag. It was an awkward maneuver to try to hide the bag behind his back, too awkward and to no avail, for Mrs. Wilps couldn't have missed seeing it.

"Going somewhere, Chewy?" she asked, giving a fish eye to that bag.

"M'mah hasn't returned yet, has she?"

"She and Mr. Wilps are at a meeting of the DAR. I don't expect them back for at least another hour." She thought Reynolds was home from his dental office awfully early for a weekday. With an overnight bag. What was up? She repeated her question.

No point in trying to deceive Mrs. Wilps, Reynolds had never gotten away with it as a child and he wouldn't get away with it now. Better to take her into his confidence.

He said, "Cloris has decided to forgive my indiscretions, well, not exactly forgive them but... Anyway, getting divorced was a mistake, we both recognize that, a serious mistake we intend to correct."

"Let me guess. You intend to re-marry. Am I right?"

"You are. We're going to drive down to West Virginia and get married again."

A sigh seemed to empty all the air from Mrs. Wilps, her bony chest seemed to go hollow. She looked up as if to question heaven and mumbled, "I get it. The sin's on me, I should'a spoke up sooner, and it won't end 'till I end it."

"What, Mrs. Wilps?"

Stephen Tannenbaum

She took hold of his arm lightly and said, "Come into the kitchen. We need to talk."

"I'm in a bit of a hurry right now. We're on a tight schedule."

"Please, Chewy, for me?"

"You know ordinarily I'd do anything for you, Mrs. Wilps, but…"

"Listen, dear boy. Now don't get me wrong, I have nothing mean to say about your mama and her DAR and her Garden Club and her Young Republican Women and her Environmental Collective and all the rest; nothing good about them, if you ask me, but nothing bad either. But while she was lording it over all of them, I was the closest thing to a mother you ever really had, so I'm asking, for me, come into the kitchen and we'll talk."

We will talk or *you* will? Reynolds wondered ruefully. But that settled it. He remembered countless times when Mrs. Wilps had taken him into her kitchen, kissed the boo-boo, the place on him that had hurt, and made him hot chocolate. He did not, could not resist being tugged toward the kitchen. The kitchen, after all, was as much familiar ground to him as it was to Mrs. Wilps. It had often been a sanctuary.

She led him to the tiny round table in a corner between the pantry door and the onion bin, the table at which he had been fed many times as an infant, as a child, as a young man. She sat him there now and pulled up a second chair to face him.

She looked approvingly around the familiar surroundings. She said, "This place is mine, my kitchen. I don't own it, of course, but it's mine nonetheless, and by the grace of God and the Hughes family, it'll be mine until the day I die. I might decide to haunt it afterwards."

Reynolds said, "It'll always be yours, if I have anything to say about it, Mrs. Wilps." He was willing to spare a few minutes to placate her, but he was so anxious to get moving and for her to get to the point, if she had one—he was having trouble sitting still.

She continued, "And when I'm not here in the kitchen I'm upstairs making the beds, vacuuming the carpets, dusting the furniture. Or I'm in the basement washing and ironing the clothes."

"So?"

"My point is, I'm a servant, Chewy. Mr. Wilps and me, we're servants."

"I don't think of you that way."

"Regardless, we are, we're servants. And you know what they say about servants: we see and hear everything that goes on under the roof. I mean to say it's true, I've seen and heard everything that's gone on under this roof since the day I was first employed, before you were born."

She had seen and heard everything since day one, and she was able to add one and one and come up with two, "…whereas some people, smart as they are…"

She poked him in the ribs with a stiff finger. "… can't seem to see beyond the tip of their nose."

Reynolds didn't doubt she was right about that, and seeing Mrs. Wilps begin to count the facts on her fingers felt like heartburn. He guessed he wasn't going to like what he was about to hear.

She said, "Number one, you know your father had a fling with a woman or two, maybe even three, before he married your mama. And, number two, that one of those women happened to be your Cloris's mother, Katherine Schermer. Number three…"

Reynolds said, "I'm not going to like this, am I, Mrs. Wilps?"

Mrs. Wilps shook her head.

"No, I'm sure you're not gonna. But that doesn't change a thing. Now, number three: You know your grandfather convinced your father to throw over the girl he was most serious about in order to marry your mama. Number four, you know that after the throw-over your grandfather or your father, prolly both, gave Katherine Schermer a house to live in."

"Yes, for one dollar. The house on Harrison Avenue. Cloris found the deed."

"The very one. Now, Chewy, what does one, two, three and four add up to?"

"I was sure I wasn't going to like this, and I don't."

"Chewy…"

"Alright, Yes, it adds up to... and I think I kind of knew this all along, but I think I repressed it."

"My momma—Lord rest her—used to call it willful ignorance."

"It adds up, doesn't it? At the time of the throwover, Katherine Schermer must have been, was... I wish it were otherwise but, oh, she was, she had to have been... She pretty much had to have been, right? She had to have been pregnant, correct? With, it was with Cloris, wasn't it?"

"Gold star for your forehead, sweetie."

"This is awful, Mrs. Wilps," Reynolds said.

He had had enough, but there was more.

She said, "What do we conclude from all this, knowing, as we do, that Cloris's supposed father, Jack Schermer, might be—to quote your mother—just might just be a fiction? What do we conclude from that and all the rest?"

Reynolds looked as if Mrs. Wilps had rapped him on the head with a rolling pin. "That P'pah... Oh. That Cloris is..."

"Yes."

Later, Reynolds sat behind the wheel of his BMW, the car idling, the driver no longer anxious to get on the road, his previous tight schedule having been considerably loosened. His overnight bag sat beside him in the passenger's bucket seat, looking hopelessly futile and somewhat intimidating. He wondered if he ought to have abandoned it in Worthington Manor.

He wound slowly downhill and turned left toward the Downtown and the flower shop, where Cloris was waiting. What was he to tell Cloris? How to even broach the subject?

How perverse the human brain, he thought, when almost immediately he was able to conjure up an image of how he might go about broaching the subject:

He imagined the automatic door chime of *Posies* cheerfully chiming to announce his entry into the shop; next he imagined himself flippantly calling out to Cloris, "Hey, Sis!"

Oh, God. He pulled over to the curb, he was about to lose his lunch.

CHAPTER 22

A Greek Tragedy

The door chime greeted his entrance into *Posies*, just as Reynolds had imagined it would, but there the scenario ended: there would not be any kind of cheerful shout to Cloris. Reynolds was in no shouting mood. His mouth tasted of vomit, his stomach was turning somersaults and his heart ached, for himself and for her. Besides which, the woman standing behind the counter fussing over a dozen yellow roses in a tall glass vase was not Cloris. It was Edwina Tipson.

Mrs. Tipson was the epitome of everybody's third grade teacher, a beanpole of a farm woman with mousy hair in a bun at the back of her head, and what Reynolds assumed were false teeth set in a permanent desperate smile. Except that in Reynolds' case, his third-grade teacher had not been afflicted, as Mrs. Tipson was, with rheumatoid arthritis to the extent that her hands were bound up in knots and her spine looked as if it were intent on folding in half.

"Well, Dr. Hughes. About time, isn't it? Cloris waited and waited. Nervous as a cat, she was. Wondering what on earth was keeping you."

Reynolds was too young to have heard the voice of Eleanor Roosevelt, but he had heard imitators, and he thought Mrs. Tipson's voice was a pretty good imitation.

She continued, her voice often skipping octaves, "I expected you'd turn up sooner or later." From the disapproving look she aimed his way, Reynolds could tell that the old lady disapproved of a man keeping his wife waiting. Or in this case his ex-wife.

"I was held up, Mrs. Tipson," he said. When that seemed to alarm her, he added, "I mean I was delayed. I take it Cloris is no longer here?"

"Correct. Anxious as she was, she was making me nervous. I sent her to make a delivery, an anniversary, the Loughners are having their twenty-first and right in your neighborhood, too. I mean they live in your…"

"I know the Loughners."

"Well, of course you do, dear boy. Cloris was as anxious to get out of here as I was to get her out. The delivery was as good an excuse as any. Irises, it was, and day lilies, beautiful day lilies. I don't think she could stand waiting here another minute. Cloris, I mean, not Mrs. Loughner. And she said she would wait for you at home in Larchmont. Cloris will, not Mrs.…."

Reynolds was getting dizzy. He said goodbye to Mrs. Tipson and left the shop. Retrieved his car from where he had parked it at the yellow curb in front of the *Juice 'n Java*, and aimed the *BMW* out of the Downtown, toward their home in Larchmont.

On the way he found it necessary to pull over alongside a roadside culvert; having already emptied his stomach, he merely dry heaved. He felt less like the indomitable, resolute Hughes man—physically or mentally—than he had ever felt in his life. His stomach persisted its upheaval, his head was a swirling confusion and his heart was a jumble of emotions. He felt as if he had been roughed up by forces out of his control; felt as if he had been kicked around by capricious Gods, like Sophocles's Oedipus in the ancient Greek tragedies he had read at Princeton. Fate's treatment of him was downright Oedipal, and like that luckless character of myth, he was angry and confused. What had he done to deserve this? Or Cloris, what had she done? But then he realized that along with anger and confusion, he also felt a rush of relief. At least the truth was finally out.

As he turned onto their street, he passed without really noticing the green pickup truck of Maestromateo the Gardener. Mattie, working in the front yard of a neighbor across the street, recognized Reynolds' red *BMW* and waved to it. Got no response.

Reynolds turned into the driveway, used the remote, pulled into the garage, parked. He sat behind the wheel for a while, wishing he could think of some way to spare Cloris some of the shock and pain he had gone through, but if such a way existed, he had yet to think of it. He hadn't even thought of a gentle way to broach the subject with her.

He needn't have wasted time trying to spare her, his face was a mirror of his feelings, and since it was the face Cloris had come to love, she was able to read trouble on it as easily as if his face were the front page of the *County Tribune*.

The banner headline she read on page one of his face: DISASTER STRIKES!

It was the absence of the *'I'm in Command'* look she had always seen in Reynolds' eyes, and the tiny lines of distress between them, that told Cloris she was in for a disappointment. The proud set of his shoulders was gone as well. Right away she thought she knew.

They faced each other across the kitchen, he standing near the door from the garage, she in the middle of the kitchen with her back braced against the central island. Unable to think of anything rational to say, Cloris blurted out the first thing that came to mind: that she had delivered flowers to their neighbors, the Loughners.

"It's their anniversary, the twenty-something, I forget which."

Reynolds said that he knew that, Mrs. Tipson had told him.

She said, "You were taking so long, I couldn't figure out why. I was starting to lose it, so Edwina..."

He knew all about that too and he apologized for the delay. He had packed a few things to take along to West Virginia, he told her, and was about to leave Worthington Manor when she insisted they have a little talk.

Cloris said, clenching a fist, "I think I'm going to punch my mother-in-law."

"No no, Cloris, not M'mah. I was referring to Mrs. Wilps."

"Mrs. Wilps? Your nanny?"

"My nanny, the housekeeper, the cook, the laundress, everything in one. Mrs. Wilps, who claims to have seen all and heard all since before I was born. She guessed we were going to re-marry, and before we did, she insisted on telling me some things."

"Things? What things?"

"Well, actually, she didn't have to tell them to me, I mean I kind of already knew them, but I had repressed them. Things that I really knew but didn't want to face. Mrs. Wilps thinks you kind of know them too, Cloris, but don't want to face them. Willful ignorance, she calls it."

Cloris felt that Mrs. Wilps was right about one thing, she didn't want to face them, whatever they were. She said, "Like...what?"

Reynolds thought, *What was the use of not coming*

right out with it? He said, "Like, you're probably my sister."

Whatever reaction Reynolds expected from Cloris failed to materialize; she seemed curiously unaffected. He wondered if she had known all along, or had at least suspected. He was knocked off balance by her reply to what he had thought was shocking news.

She said, "Oh, well. And here I thought you were going to say our trip to West Virginia was off. You know what? I feel like a cup of coffee."

The back door bell interrupted them as Reynolds was about to reply. Cloris turned to the cabinet that held the makings for coffee, leaving Reynolds, still feeling off balance, to answer the door bell.

He opened the kitchen door to find the gardener, Bruno Maestromateo, standing there. The two men had not been formally introduced—Mattie's business had always been with Cloris, whom he referred to as the Missus—but there was no mistaking the elderly man who smelled of mown grass and compost, who was dressed in dusty denim coveralls, wore Iron City work boots and a peaked ball cap as anyone but the gardener. At the same time Mattie was not likely to mistake the man of the house, who paid the bills in full and on time. Nor had he missed the red *BMW*.

Mattie had three decades on Reynolds; he also had an inherent Italian indifference to authority. These notwithstanding, Mattie removed the ball cap when he said, "Dr. Hughes."

Reynolds, taken aback by the old man's formality, was sorry he had no hat to doff. Instead he nodded and replied, "Mr. Maestromateo, I presume."

An awkward moment arose when both men thought they ought to shake hands. Mattie took a look at his right hand and thought to wipe it on his pants leg before offering it to Reynolds, who by that time had given up on the idea.

He said, "What can we do for you, Mr...."

"I'm called by everyone, Mattie."

"Well, what can we do for you, Mr. Mattie?"

"I'm please talk with the Missus," Mattie said.

Reynolds said, "Your timing really sucks, but..."

"I'm here, Mattie," Cloris called from her spot by the coffee maker. "Come in, have coffee with us."

Reynolds backed away from his position blocking Mattie's way. He said, frowning, "Sure, come in."

"No, Missus," Mattie said as he entered the kitchen, "I drink coffee now, I don't sleep tonight." He fell silent until he realized they were waiting for him. "I'm hunting nurseries all over for just the right tree to replace the dead yew."

Reynolds heard 'Hughes' and was startled. "There aren't many Hugheses left, which one died?"

Cloris had completely forgotten about the dead yew. She corrected her ex-husband, "Not a Hughes, a yew. Y-E-W. A tree, an evergreen. Haven't you noticed the hole in the corner of the yard where the yew used to be?" She showed him the spot by pointing out the window over the kitchen sink. But no, he hadn't noticed.

Mattie continued, "I found him in a place near Ligonier, a beauty of a blue spruce. The right height, the shape a just so…" He drew a huge spreading shape on the air. "…And such color, dark, dark green and blue like a steel. I bring him tomorrow for you to approve of him."

"A tree from Ligonier, eh? Sure, Mr. Mattie," Reynolds said, "you do that, you bring him…"

"No," Cloris said, pronouncing it emphatically, "Mattie, no. Dr. Hughes and I are going out of town tomorrow, we've got business to attend to in West Virginia, and we…"

"But Cloris…"

"…And we won't be back for a day, maybe two. Could you bring the tree, say, Friday? We…"

"We can't, can we, Cloris?"

"We can, we can be back by Friday."

"I didn't mean that, I meant…"

Mattie said, "Friday is a good day for planting him. I bring him then."

"I don't think we should…" Reynolds.

"Good, then that's settled. We'll see you and the new tree on Friday." Cloris hugged the gardener's arm to her, led him to the kitchen door and outside.

After escorting Mattie as far as the patio, Cloris returned to the kitchen; she was all smiles and she was dusting off her hands as if she had just finished clearing off her entire to-do list.

She said, "There now, see?"

Reynolds said, "See what?"

Cloris said, "To Mattie, nothing has changed. You're *Dr.* Hughes, I'm *Missus* Hughes. The world is turning at the same speed as before, nobody is falling off, nobody is going to fall off."

"You're not making sense, Cloris."

"I am too. I'm saying, nobody is making a Greek tragedy of this except you, and nobody is going to. We were married once, weren't we? Were we siblings then?"

"Well, yes, we were." He got a hard look from Cloris that made him concede, "Okay, probably. We were *probably* siblings."

"Nobody knew then and nobody cared."

Reynolds said, "Nobody asked. If they'd asked…"

"Nobody asked then and nobody will ask now. But if anybody should happen to ask, we're the Hugheses, and that's exactly who we are. If we act like a married couple is expected to, who'll be any the wiser?"

He said, "But we'll have to lie when we fill out the paperwork in West Virginia."

Cloris said, shaking her head, "If we have to lie, we'll lie. It won't be the first time anybody's ever done that, and it won't be the last."

Just when Cloris thought she had him convinced, Reynolds looked doubtful once again.

He said, "All that time, Cloris, we were trying to get you pregnant, we worried something was wrong with us. What dumb luck. But now…"

She said, "Not to worry. I'm on *The Pill*, have been since you moved out."

"So, we don't have to worry about…"

"About anything, sweetie," Cloris said, up on tip toes hugging her arms around his waist, "We don't have a worry in the world."

CHAPTER 23

Breathing

Had the Earth somehow sped up in its orbit around the sun, shortening the night and bringing the morning more quickly on? As if eager to get underway? It seemed so to Cloris. She was reluctant to let the night go, so deep and untroubled had her sleep been, like that of an innocent child. Yet she eagerly greeted the morning, knowing that the man who lay next to her, the man who *had* been her husband would soon be her husband again.

Now they were both up and dressed for the drive south to West Virginia, overnight bags were packed and waiting by the kitchen door. They were breakfasting on coffee and toasted muffins with strawberry jam.

Reynolds said, "I figure we'll take Interstate 70 west and later switch to Route 19 south. That's a straight shot down to Beckley."

Cloris's brow went up. She said, "You've been planning."

"I have, yes, and I'm pretty sure I 70 and Route 19 is the quickest way."

Cloris said, "But that old State road can be a bottleneck, with cars and 18-wheelers and, Christ, even tractors. Remember? We were stuck on that road once."

"Yes, but it was in the middle of the afternoon. This time of the morning, it's likely the fastest way to Beckley, and Beckley is our best chance to get married today, without delay. We don't want any further delays, do we?"

Cloris shook her head and washed down a bit of muffin with coffee. Something overnight had managed to change his mind about remarrying; she wondered what it was.

"I didn't change my mind."

"Umhm, you did. Yesterday you weren't convinced remarrying was the right thing to do. Now you're all for it and in a hurry about it."

"So, okay, I changed my mind." Reynolds dipped the tip of his finger in the jam jar and licked it off. Not an elegant delaying tactic, but he needed a moment to think. He finally said, "I didn't sleep as well as you did last night. I lay awake a lot, listening to you breathe. I lay awake listening to your breathing and worrying that our plan to remarry was in defiance of the law, in defiance of everybody's religion, in defiance of everything legal and sacred. Now, for sure, Hughes men never put any trust in god and never feared him.

And we never held anything sacred except for the Almighty Dollar, but still…

"But I lay awake listening to your breathing until I swear, I was almost hypnotized by the sound of it. I tried to adjust the rhythm of my own breathing to yours, and when I finally achieved that, when our breathing was in perfect sync, I felt so satisfied, so clean and glad. Being right beside you, in harmony, my breathing in sync with yours, well, I realized that was the way it was meant to be."

Reynolds said, "I did finally fall asleep, but not before I was convinced that *we* were meant to be. I say, to hell with everybody else and their opinions, and that's all there is to it."

Cloris promised herself that she would keep on breathing, if that's what it took. She said, "You're sure now?"

"I'm sure now." He looked at the clock on the wall above them. "It's time to hit the road."

Cloris looked at him and smiled. "Yes, it's time."

She stood, collected their breakfast things, put them in the sink, left them un-rinsed.

She said, "Let's go. Whose car, yours or mine?"

CHAPTER **24**

An Arbor Day

F riday morning was the kind of morning that
turns sleepyheads into early risers, one of
those rare, glorious mornings in late August
when a breeze that blows in from the north converts
breathing from something mundane into a lark. There
was a small commercial bakery close by the Hughes
house—close by if you travel the miles as the birds
and the breeze do—and at six a.m. Cloris Hughes—
that is, Mrs. Cloris Hughes, wife of Dr. Reynolds
Hughes, DMD—Cloris, in pajamas and a terry robe,
was standing on the garden patio behind the house
breathing deeply of the scents of green grass, of viburnum, of pepper bush, of marigold, petunia, and
of freshly baked bread. It promised to be a real barn
burner of an afternoon, she could feel the threat of
that in the sun on her shoulders. But for now, it was
glorious. What a morning to have your bowl of Chee-
rios with cold milk and sliced banana; what a morning
to kiss your husband and send him off to work; what
a morning to get your gardening boots wet as you

wander through dewy grass. And she thought, *What a morning to plant a tree.*

Yes, it was *an* arbor day, but not *the* Arbor Day. Not a National holiday with a capital 'A'. It was the day they all agreed that Bruno Maestromateo would bring what he promised would be the perfect replacement for the dead yew—a magnificent blue spruce, a tree that Mattie, in his inimitable way, called him.

As Mattie and his entourage threaded their way through the Larchmont neighborhood toward the Hughes house, it was as if they were on parade, though without the usual high school marching band and volunteer hose company. Admittedly it was not much of an entourage, only two vehicles: Mattie leading the way slowly in his green Ford F150 pickup, followed by a two-ton dump truck with two young Latino laborers in the cab, and in the truck bed along with a small pile of compost from Poole's Mushroom Farm stood the star attraction of this pitiful parade, the magnificent blue spruce—him.

Either by accident or by plan—who knows which or if it mattered—the parade lurched to a halt at the curb in front of the Hughes house just as the garage door rose and Reynolds emerged in the red BMW and started up the driveway.

Cloris, rinsing the breakfast dishes at the kitchen sink and looking out the window, watched as Reynolds and Mattie each dismounted from his vehicle and approached the rear of the two-ton truck. Cloris saw the two men standing next to each other, each with his hands in his pockets, each staring at the tree then at each other, at the tree then at each other: either talking to each other or silent, she couldn't tell, admiring 'him' or not she also couldn't tell. The Latino laborers watched warily and stood waiting nervously for orders. Cloris knew Reynolds disliked getting his hands dirty and that Mattie had a low opinion of anyone who preferred clean hands. That was enough of an excuse for two men to strike up a dislike for each other.

Men, she thought, shaking her head. *I'd better get out there*. Besides, she wanted to see 'him' too. She dried her hands and hurried out.

By the time Cloris arrived to take a position between the gardener and her husband, Reynolds had already said, "You're right, it's a beautiful tree..."

Mattie waited for the other shoe to drop.

"...but I must say I expected something a little bigger. It's, what, maybe four feet high?"

Mattie said, "More like five." He was insulted on the tree's behalf. He said, "Napoleon was short. *Il Duce* was short. He will grow. One day he will look down on your house."

Reynolds didn't like the sound of that or its implications. He was about to reply, but a cold look from Cloris changed his mind.

She said, "You're going to be late, Reynolds, dear.

Mrs. Tagliafaro probably has your first patient prepped and ready for surgery and…"

Reynolds looked at his watch, frowned at it.

"…and you know how upset Mrs. T gets when you fall behind schedule." He nodded. She said, "Not to worry, dear. I'll take care of things here."

Reynolds, knowing when he was outnumbered and outvoted, shrugged away any objections he might have had about the tree. He gave Cloris a peck on the cheek, nodded at the gardener, returned to his car and drove off.

Cloris and Mattie watched until the red BMW was out of sight. She placed her hand on Mattie's sleeve. She said, "Mattie, I can't tell you how grateful I am that you searched and finally found my new tree. He's absolutely gorgeous."

Indeed he was, so darkly green and blue and perfectly cone-shaped. Mattie blushed, booted a pebble across the street.

"It's got a large root ball, Mattie, a lot larger than the yew had. We've got a lot of digging to do."

We? Mattie didn't want to discourage her, knowing how much she loved to pitch in with the work, but what lay ahead was work for stronger backs than hers. Or his own. He said, "I brought these two." He nodded at his young crewmen.

Cloris said to them, "You fellas have your work cut out for you."

They both nodded vigorously at her. Big smiles.

Mattie said, "They no understand a word of English. I use Italian on them."

Cloris looked on as the men huddled and Mattie used his Italian on the young Latinos. She watched with her heart in her mouth as the three men struggled the tree off the truck bed, balanced its huge root ball precariously on a wheelbarrow and rolled it with a great deal of difficulty up the driveway, past the side of the house and into the garden.

They unloaded tools from Mattie's pickup, and with spades and a pickaxe the young men battled their way through dry earth, some shale and clay, widening the hole to accommodate the tree's big footprint.

Mattie considered what he might come up with in order to get the Missus involved in the planting. He rolled the wheelbarrow to the truck, filled it with compost and returned with it to the garden.

He said to Cloris, "We line a the hole with mushroom manure to nourish the young a roots, an old trick my Papa taught me." It sounded like a reasonable enough chore, even if he'd just made it up. With that he ceremoniously offered her a trowel.

Cloris found the aroma of mushroom manure warmed by the morning sun to be more rousing than a mug of strong coffee. She shook her head to reject the tool, and instead, on hands and knees beside the barrow, she scooped handfuls of manure and neatly packed the inside of the hole. Mattie stood behind her, ostensibly supervising the act over her shoulder. When she was finished, she looked up at the gardener; he nodded his approval.

Offloading the tree, pushing the barrow, widening the hold, lining it—all of these were hot, heavy work. The three men and Cloris sweated and grinned at each other, and admired the princely tree as it stood triumphantly in its new place in the garden. They ran a hose from a spigot on the side of the house across the garden to the tree, set the flow to a trickle, and stood by for the better part of a half hour watching the water drain down to be sucked up by the tree's eager young roots.

Cloris and the old gardener could be mistaken for worshipers as they stood reverently in front of the new tree. The young Latino laborers may not have understood any English, but they did understand that their boss and the woman he called 'Missus' preferred to be left alone. They returned to the truck and waited in the cab.

Cloris said to the old man, "Mattie, I admit, I'm worried about him. He's beautiful, true enough, but he's so vulnerable."

"I'm thinking, no," Mattie said. He turned his expert gardener's eye once again to reviewing every aspect of the installation; he nodded, satisfied.

He said, "He's in a the place where he belongs, and he knows it. No need to worry about him now, Missus. He'll be fine."

Almost as an afterthought, "Of course, I keep a careful eye on him."

Cloris nodded, wished Mattie a good rest of the day, then turned back toward the house. As she entered through the patio doors, she said quietly to herself, "I will, too, Mattie. I will, too."

The End

ABOUT THE AUTHOR

S tephen was born, raised and educated in Pittsburgh, PA. After graduating from Pitt Dental
School and serving a stint in the Army Reserve
in the mid-60's, Stephen lived, helped raise two children and practiced family dentistry in Westmoreland
County, the site of this novel, for nearly forty years.

Writing fiction has always been his second love.
He and his first love, his wife Shirley, have returned
to living in Pittsburgh.